"*I said,*" he repeated lethally soft-voiced, "*come here.*"

"I don't see why I should."

He uncoiled from his chair and moved toward her with all the contained savagery of a panther about to sprint. He was touching her again, this time with just one finger, allowing it to snake a crazy path down the side of her cheek.

With a sharply indrawn breath she allowed his fingers to slide down her neck and over the soft swell of her blouse.

She stifled a groan. "Don't, Elliot. I don't know what you think you can prove by this, but please don't."

"Move away then," he whispered maddeningly in her ear. "I'm not holding you, Rachel, you're doing this of your own accord."

It was true. His touch was featherlight, yet it held her against him like a band of tempered steel.

"You want me as much as I want you. We both know it."

SALLY HEYWOOD is a British author, born in Yorkshire. After leaving university, she had several jobs, including running an art gallery, a guest house and a boutique. She has written several plays for theater and television, in addition to her romance novels for Harlequin. Her special interests are sailing, reading, fashion, interior decorating and helping in a children's nursery.

Books by Sally Heywood

Don't miss any of our special offers. Write to us at the following address for information on our newest releases.

Harlequin Reader Service
P.O. Box 1397, Buffalo, NY 14240
Canadian address: P.O. Box 603,
Fort Erie, Ont. L2A 5X3

SALLY HEYWOOD

Steps to Heaven

Harlequin Books

TORONTO • NEW YORK • LONDON
AMSTERDAM • PARIS • SYDNEY • HAMBURG
STOCKHOLM • ATHENS • TOKYO • MILAN
MADRID • WARSAW • BUDAPEST • AUCKLAND

Harlequin Presents first edition January 1993
ISBN 0-373-11521-0

Original hardcover edition published in 1991
by Mills & Boon Limited

STEPS TO HEAVEN

CHAPTER ONE

RACHEL placed the wig on the model's head as a final touch then stepped back. Her mind wasn't really on her job—she was still thinking about last night—but she forced herself to concentrate on what she was doing and adjusted the position of the model's hand to a more elegant pose. The silvery tresses of the wig were just fine. Really dramatic with the black day dress the model had on, she thought. Maybe if she asked Lulu, the chief window dresser, she might be able to borrow the wig when this week's display was finished. It would be just right for what she wanted.

'Hurry up, Rachel. Are you asleep?' It was Lyn, the girl with the accessories. 'Like this hat?' she asked, coming into the window area and placing a wide-brimmed garden party hat on top of the model's head.

'Where would you wear a hat like that?' Rachel brought herself back to the present with an effort.

'Ascot?' It was June and the races were coming up the following week; the store was full of women shoppers splurging on eye-catching outfits suitable for the Royal Enclosure.

'Ascot?' exclaimed Rachel. 'We should be so lucky. We'll be here, slaving away all week as usual.' She gave a yawn.

'Late night?' Lyn was already busy matching bags and scarves to the display as Rachel turned to go.

In reply she merely nodded. Shyness made her reluctant to admit where she had been and what she
had been up to for the last three nights. If things
worked out she would tell Lyn and everyone else
before long. She would even, she crossed her
fingers, be handing in her notice. If things worked
out.

'Lulu?' she asked when she reached the staff
refreshment-room and found the head of their
group just coming in for a cup of coffee. 'What
happens to the wigs when the displays are finished
with?'

'They go back to the store-room. Why?'

'And just lie about on the shelves, gathering
dust?'

'I suppose so.'

'Then I don't suppose there's any chance I could
borrow one, is there?'

'To wear, you mean?'

Rachel nodded, suddenly blushing. It sounded
ridiculous now. Lulu would think she was crackers.

But the older girl grinned. 'I get it. You're going
to a fancy-dress party? You youngsters always start
looking at the displays when there are parties in the
offing.'

Rachel continued to look hopeful.

'If you're very careful I don't see why not—so
long as you ask me first—and Rachel,' Lulu paused,
'don't spread the word around. I'm not really supposed to do it.'

Rachel had already guessed she had created quite
a good impression at work and now she had proof.
'I'll be really careful. Lulu,' she added impulsively,
'you are sweet.' Then she bit her lip. 'It isn't just

a one-off thing though; I meant, could I borrow it
for a couple of nights or maybe even longer?'

'Your social life!' She obviously thought Rachel
intended to wear it at a succession of parties. 'How
long did you say you'd been in London?'

Rachel's oval face broke into a smile and she put
on a country accent. 'I been oop from t'farm these
three months past,' she joked.

It was true, she thought as she took a quick coffee
break and went back to do a shoe display on the
first floor. Three months. But, contrary to thinking
it was a short time like Lulu, she was conscious of
every minute passing and getting no nearer her goal.
Until this week.

Her secret ambition was something no one in the
world knew about, and the plans she had laid in
order to fulfil what seemed like a wild dream had
only begun to fall into place when her parents had
given permission for her to leave home. They had
demurred at first, Mrs Jackson believing that
twenty was too young for a girl on her own in
London and Mr Jackson going along with whatever
his wife said, until, as luck would have it, one of
Rachel's school friends had got a place on a catering
course in London. Not wishing to go up alone and
knowing Rachel was keen to go, she'd asked her if
she would like to share a flat until they both found
their feet.

A further stroke of luck from Rachel's point of
view was when she managed to get a job as window
dresser with a large Knightsbridge store. She had
done the same job in the Dorset town close to where
she lived after doing a training stint at the local art
and technical college.

'Surely you can't have any objections now, Mum,' she'd pleaded when the plan was mooted. 'Ros is as sensible and reliable a flatmate as anybody could wish for.' If she'd exaggerated slightly in order to plead her cause it wasn't too far from the truth, and Mrs Jackson had finally given in, though not without a promise that Rachel would come straight home if things didn't turn out well.

'You'll be back, my lass,' she'd said as she bustled around the big farmhouse kitchen. 'You'll be missing your friends, and the horses, and the choir and the village carnival. Country things are best. You'll learn London streets are paved the same as anywhere else.'

But Rachel had taken to London as if she had been born and bred in the city. Not that she didn't miss the farm and her friends and all the country sights and sounds, but she consoled herself with long walks in the park, grateful that the flat Ros's London uncle had offered them in a part of his Regency terraced house was just five minutes from the sight of trees and grass.

But, despite all the excitement of settling in a new place, right up until last week she had felt she was merely marking time. Then her big break had come.

'Rachel! Wake up! You're miles away!' It was one of her friends on the perfume counter. 'I asked you if you wanted to try a spray of this.' She held up a sample of expensive perfume and Rachel came to with a start.

'Sorry, I was just thinking!' She held out a wrist.

'Is he gorgeous?'

'Who?' Rachel blinked her blue eyes, then gave a little laugh when she understood what Francine meant. 'I was *not* dreaming about a man, thank you very much! No time for those!'

'No time? Why, whatever else can you be up to?' Francine waited, obviously expecting all to be revealed, but Rachel, despite the urge to blurt out what she was 'up to', refrained from telling her, saying only, 'Getting used to life in the big city, Francine, that's what I mean!'

In a waft of expensive perfume she made her way back towards the escalator. With all her dreaminess today she was a little behind schedule, and after a quick look at her watch she began to fume at the slowness of the customers as they plodded in front of her. Usually she felt sorry for them, having to lug heavy shopping-bags around with them and with only a limited time to enjoy the merchandise on display when she herself could stroll round at leisure after the store was closed, picking and choosing in her imagination what she might buy—if only she could have afforded the expensive goods on sale.

But this morning she was in too much of a hurry to dawdle among the shoppers; her head was still buzzing after the previous night and besides she was behind schedule. And that meant she would be late getting back to the flat. And in turn that gave her less time to go over her songs beforehand.

She dodged round a group of women and children but came slap up against the store manager conducting a party of men in suits. Directors, she judged, looking at their briefcases and serious expressions.

She reached the staff lift just before they did and was surprised when they followed her in. Mr Maynard ignored her, as did the other men, and she found herself crushed in a corner, making her scowl behind a wall of dark backs. When she glanced up, a pair of deep blue eyes caught her own and gave a flash of sympathy. The man's lips tightened in an attempt not to laugh and he turned away, giving her adequate time to inspect his profile as the lift travelled softly between floors. He was certainly worth looking at, she though idly, for once torn away from thoughts of the evening ahead.

The men were obviously going up to the boardroom on the top floor and Rachel had to push her way as firmly as she could towards the doors without seeming to appear rude, a seemingly impossible task until the blue-eyed stranger murmured something to the men next to him and they parted to let her through. She shot a brief glance of gratitude at him as she slipped through the silently opening doors. Then she forgot him.

There was a smell of something delicious coming from the kitchen when she finally reached home that evening. Throwing off her shoes in the hallway, she sniffed the air appreciatively and went through.

'There's certainly something to be said for sharing a flat with a catering student. What are you concocting tonight, Ros?'

The dark-haired girl looked up, rather pink in the face from having just been peering anxiously inside the old-fashioned electric oven. 'Wait and see! It's a surprise!'

Rachel pottered around the kitchen, helping where she could, but in reality her mind was miles away.

The thing for which she lived was drawing closer. Only another three hours! Then she would be treading the stage! She imagined the trio striking up with her special tune, the one she had written herself, and the gradual hush that would fall over the audience. Then Rachel Jackson, junior window dresser, would exist no more! Her practical, workaday garb of jumper and jeans would be replaced by a glittery tube of diamanté and her straight mouse hair would be caught up in a clip which, from the front tables, should look like diamonds. Rachel would become Zia. And then she would begin to sing and the bliss of knowing the audience seemed to like what she did would sweep over her. She gave a contented sigh at the prospect.

'My stage fright hasn't come yet,' she remarked, as she washed her hands and started to get on with laying the table. 'It really hasn't.'

But it did. Halfway through supper she pushed back her plate. 'I'm sorry, Ros, it's nothing to do with your cooking. But I feel dreadful. I'll have to put this in the fridge for tomorrow.'

'It'll be ruined.' Ros wasn't offended. She had seen Rachel on previous nights, seen how pale she suddenly became, and how her hands started to shake. She had pushed her food away then as well, even though she had already admitted to being ravenous after a busy day at the store.

Ros tried without success to jolly her out of it but it was no good, her stage fright stayed with Rachel all the time she was sitting in the taxi as it took her into the West End, and it stayed all the time she was getting changed and putting up her hair and applying her stage make-up, and it wasn't until she stepped into the pool of silver light and gazed out at last into the darkness surrounding the stage and began to sing the first throbbing notes of her opening ballad that it finally left her.

It was then the excitement took over, the alert attention telling of the audience's least change of mood. The first time she had felt it she had been surprised. But in three short evenings she had come to expect it, to love it, to find herself reading it and playing to it, structuring her songs to fit the mood, playing on their sense of expectation as if she could tease them into giving her their approval, then, having it, turning it into a spiral of happiness to match the happiness that bubbled up inside her until at last the music died and the lights faded.

Tonight she collapsed in her dressing-room, pleasurably exhausted, until the manager came through as he had done the previous nights. He was smiling. 'That was a lovely set, Zia. Listen!' He held the dressing-room door open. In the distance she could hear the applause continuing like the fall of surf on a distant beach. He turned back. 'You're going to have to give them one more.'

She moved in a dream, back into the spotlight, stage fright forgotten. This time the lights were glowing softly over the tables and for the first time she could see individual faces in the audience. It was slightly unnerving but she turned to the band and took up the cue and in a moment she was launching into a popular love-song, aware of the eyes on her, of being the centre of attention, and not frightened at all.

*   *   *

When she eventually returned to the flat Ros was just getting ready for bed. She made two mugs of cocoa and, handing one to Rachel and noting her starry-eyed look, said, 'I always knew you were special when we were at school. I'm really pleased things are working out for you.' She looked thoughtful. 'I have to say though, love, I think you're making a mistake in cutting yourself off from ordinary life. You can't work all the time. You need a social life as well ... Everybody needs people, Rachel.'

'By people I suppose you mean *men*?'

'Singular. A special man. You never go out. Now you're at the club you're singing there every night and when you're not singing you're rehearsing. You won't meet any nice men like that.'

Rachel could see the concern in her friend's eyes but her lips tightened fractionally. 'I've ruled out social life for the time being, Ros. And I'm certainly not looking for a husband! He would only get in the way. I'm sure you'll be able to run a career and be a good wife if it comes to it, but it's not for me. There's no way I could dedicate myself to my career and have spare time for anything else. I need to be free, not have a husband hanging round my neck! I'm going to have to be free to travel, to tour ... I couldn't give one hundred per cent to a relationship until I'm established. It's one or the other.'

'All or nothing?'

'Yes, I suppose so.'

'Do you realise what you're giving up?'

'I'm not giving anything up.' For some reason a brief image of a pair of laughing blue eyes floated

in front of her and she gave a little shrug of annoyance. 'I don't look at it like that.' She finished
her cocoa. 'I'm giving nothing up at all. Now I
really must go to bed. I'm dog-tired.'

That was the end of the matter as far as she was
concerned. Next morning when she went in to work
all her thoughts were on what Ray, the manager of
the club, had said to her the previous night. 'I want
to put you under contract, love. You're too good
to lose to any passing booking agent just yet.'

'You gave me my first chance, Ray. I wouldn't
dream of leaving you so soon,' she had replied.

'You will do one day. And it's my guess it won't
be far into the future, either. You're going to be
big, love. You're a natural. If I was into singer-
management I'd get you on my books straight
away.'

'You're a flatterer, Ray,' she remembered saying,
but her heart had begun to dance at his words.
Could it be true? Certainly she had seen how the
audience reacted.

Ray had concluded by asking her to come in early
to look over a short contract he had had written
up. 'For six weeks,' he told her. 'That suit you?'

When she nodded he went on, 'If nothing has
turned up for you by then, I expect I'll be more
than willing to renew it.'

It was then she knew she could hand in her notice
at the store. Six weeks, possibly longer? He was
paying her far more than the store, though admit-
tedly she got a large discount on any goods pur-
chased plus paid holidays and sick-leave too.

She was mulling the problem over when she got
into work, clocking on at the staff entrance and

pressing the lift button semi-automatically after three months of doing the same thing every morning. Slightly late, she was pleased when it came down straight away, and she was just about to punch in her floor number when a voice called across the foyer, 'Hold it, will you?'

Such was its note of authority she automatically put out a hand to hold back the door, then glanced across to see who had called. A tall, muscular shape in a dark suit shouldered his way inside.

'Thanks.' A well-shaped hand raked through a head of dark hair, as if the owner had left in too much of a rush to groom it properly and now regretted his haste.

Such thick dark waves on a man were very unusual, Rachel remembered thinking before she found her eyes drawn towards the same pair of blue eyes that had impinged momentarily on her thoughts the day before.

'Don't you use the directors' lift?' she remarked, blurting the first thing that came into her head as her mouth went suddenly dry. He not only had outrageously sexy eyes, with a smile to match; he was also, on closer inspection and in full face, as dishy as her curious glance had revealed yesterday when she had glimpsed him in profile during that short journey between floors with his colleagues. Now, close up, she judged him too young to be a director, for he was surely no more than thirty? Thirty-two at the very outside. The same as her brother, Mark. But there all similarity ended.

He had already made some sort of reply to her blurted question, but such was her state of mind that she missed what he said and had to ask him to repeat it.

'I still don't know my way around,' he said with a quirk of firm lips that irrationally claimed her attention then.

'You walked straight past it,' she babbled, feeling weak at the knees. It's true, she registered, it does affect the knees. Literally. It? she asked herself. She turned away and frowned at the floor indicator. What on earth was she doing, reacting like an idiot to a mere *man*? A hand came down over the push-button as the lift slowed at the floor she wanted and she felt it increase speed again, going up.

'What the——?' She turned angrily. 'I'm going to be late. Why did you do that?'

Instead of being worried by her obvious anger he laughed quietly. 'I'm not as lost as I pretended just now. I saw you getting into this lift so I thought I'd take my chance while I had it.'

'What on *earth* do you mean?'

'I mean, I didn't want to lose you a second time.'

'But this is ridiculous!' She gazed at him in astonishment then let her glance slide to the floor indicator again. 'You're making me later than I already am! And just so you can chat me up!' She was genuinely angry, both with herself and with him for the way he was making her feel.

'I couldn't let you go a second time without finding out where you fitted in. This place is vast. I might not see you again for weeks.'

'You may not anyway,' she muttered furiously, her mind fleeting back to the thought that she would be handing in her notice soon.

The lift stopped again and he held his hand over the buttons. She felt it start to descend but before she could say anything, he said. 'Too efficient, this thing, isn't it? I'll have to suggest we put in a slower one. Now, what exactly do you mean by that last remark?'

But she had turned on him in fury. 'I don't know who the hell you are, but somebody in authority is going to hear about this! How am I going to explain why I'm so late? It's outrageous! Now let me out of this lift.'

He was laughing softly. 'A face as cool as rain and a temper like a little spitfire. Who'd have thought it?'

'I *never* lose my temper,' she flared.

'Never?' he broke in with a throaty chuckle.

'Only when I'm provoked,' she snapped. 'Now take your hand off the control and let me out. I mean what I say. You haven't heard the last of this!'

'What a clawy little creature you are!' The thought seemed to delight him, and his Prussian blue eyes sparked approval, lingering over her face in a way that could only be described as suggestive.

'Look, I'm going to get the sack because of you!' She felt like hitting him and he must have suddenly realised how serious she was, for his expression changed.

'I'm sorry, I didn't intend to get you into trouble. My thoughtlessness. I still haven't got used to the strict regimen here.'

'You will!' she muttered darkly.

He gave a non-committal smile. 'Not if I can help it.'

'Then you'll be out on your ear.'

He ignored that and, hand still pressed over the door control, demanded, *'Well?'*

'Well what?'

'Aren't you going to ask my name so you can report me?'

'No.' She scowled. 'You know full well I'm not going to cause trouble—provided you open the doors right now.'

'And if I don't?' He looked as if he was about to press the ascent button again.

She grabbed hold of his wrist and tried to get to the control first, and to her surprise, instead of making a scuffle of it, he moved back with a little inclination of his dark head and her hands fell to her sides, burning where she had felt the touch of his wrist.

'I'm sorry. You have every right to get out. I was simply hoping for a longer talk. What about lunch?'

'With *you*?' She gave him a slow, appraising look, feeling safe now that the doors were opening and she was already half out of them. It enabled her to prolong one of her haughtiest stares. 'I wouldn't have lunch with you,' she declared, as she looked him up and down, 'if you were the last man on earth!' He was standing with his hand held over the rubber guard on the doors.

'You're extremely sure about that,' he remarked, his eyes, his blue eyes, glinting dangerously as they suddenly swept her from top to toe in a mirroring of the arctic glance she was giving him.

'You bet I'm sure.'

'You *will* have lunch with me,' he said quietly.

She gaped at him. 'Want to bet?' Then she spun on her heel and stalked off, conscious, even as she did so, of the stranger's blue stare following her along the corridor. When she reached the door she couldn't help turning, just to make sure. He raised his hand in a small gesture of farewell as if he'd been waiting for just that backward glance and, conscious of his eyes raking her trim form in its figure-hugging jeans and plain pink sweater, she tilted her chin and pushed her way blindly through the door, feeling that, despite her own coldness, he had somehow got the better of her. It was that last betraying glance that had done it.

'Sorry I'm late!' she exclaimed at once when she saw Lulu. 'The most *impossible* man got into the lift when I was coming up just now——' and briefly she explained what had detained her.

When she finished Lulu looked puzzled. 'Can't imagine who it was. Someone in men's fashions?'

'Admin, I should think,' replied Rachel. 'He was with Mr Maynard and some of the directors yesterday. I thought he was one of them at first. But he's *far* too young.' She scowled and gathered her things together. His behaviour had been too self-assured by half. 'And to crown it all,' she added, pursing her lips, 'he actually had the gall to ask me to lunch, and when I said——' She paused.

'Go on, what did you say?'

She told her.

'Goodbye, you handsome stranger!' murmured Lulu. 'But if he's as heavenly as you say he is, I for one shan't be sorry. It means *I* can be first in line!'

'Did *I* say he was heavenly?' Rachel scowled even more.

'Not in so many words,' with a little laugh Lulu turned from the mirror where she was applying lip gloss, 'but if he got behind that barrier of ice you hide behind, he must be *really* something!'

'Rubbish,' she gave a hollow laugh, 'I mean, rubbish about ice barriers and rubbish about getting through——' She stopped, confused, before adding, 'The very last thing I want is a man hanging round, clipping my wings, ordering me about and getting in the way of my career.'

'Personally I can think of nothing nicer!' Lulu snapped her make-up bag shut and gave Rachel a teasing smile.

Suddenly she could keep her secret no longer. 'Actually, Lulu, I'm not thinking about my job here. It's just that I've started to do something I've always wanted to do and somehow it doesn't leave time for anything else. You see, I've started singing in a nightclub,' she explained, 'I've always dreamed of a singing career. I want to tour. I want to make records. I want to see the world. That means men are most definitely out.'

'They don't have to be,' remarked Lulu with a worldly little smile.

'I'm not the sleep-around sort,' Rachel muttered, knowing the other girls could overhear and would think she was very old-fashioned in her attitude. But she didn't care. Maybe it was her country upbringing, but that was how she was.

She was conscious of one or two little glances between the others as she went towards the door. But she held her head high. The thought of what Ray had told her the previous night came back to restore her confidence. They might all scoff at her dedication now, but when she was a big name they would know this was how it had had to be.

The girls were clustered round the staff notice-board when she came up later that morning. There was a buzz of interest and she peered between their heads to see what it was that was causing the excitement.

'I can't read it from here,' she said. 'What's happened?'

'Listen,' said someone at the front. '"In order to extend a welcome to the new member of the board of directors, and to facilitate more contact between the various levels of employees, staff are invited to an informal buffet luncheon on Tuesday the eleventh inst. at twelve-thirty prompt. Signed,"' as you might have guessed from its pompous tones——' the girl turned with a smile '—"The managing director, Mr Hilda Maynard."'

'Good old Hilda.'

'I'm shocked to hear you call our respected boss by any name but his own,' Lulu reprimanded them, then she spoilt the effect by bursting into laughter. 'I bet he's livid. More contact between the various levels! That's the last thing he'll want. He loves to feel he's sitting with the gods up on that top floor. He won't want the underlings encroaching!'

'New brooms sweep clean. It must be the idea of this new man. They say he's a nephew of the chairman.'

'Obviously he's got the power to bring staff re-lations into the twentieth century,' Lyn remarked. 'I must say I like the idea of the buffet lunch. It'll make a change from sandwiches or fighting shoppers for service in the crush bar.'

'I wonder what he's like,' mused Francine. 'I haven't seen him around yet. Has anybody?'

'Obviously he's going to make his debut on Wednesday when we all present ourselves for inspection.' Lulu gave a dry smile. She'd been with the store for two or three years and enjoyed the prestige of working there but never failed to point out how out of date she thought it was in its attitude to staff. She had a continual battle with the buyer for Couture, urging her to go for new, young designers instead of sticking with the more expensive and traditional ones, but to no avail.

Rachel shrugged off her jacket and hung it up. Her decision to hand in her notice was still on her mind and she couldn't feel part of everything any more, knowing her days here were numbered. It was just a question of taking the plunge. Maybe she would give it another month. It would be nice to have two salaries for a time so that she would have the money to fit herself out with a wardrobe suitable for her new role.

She asked Lulu's advice when they all began to separate to their different departments. 'I need a good, strong image for Zia—and the clothes to fit in with it,' she added.

The girls clustered round, pleased to seize on this new topic, but by the time they went down to their separate floors Lulu had taken the matter into her own hands.

'I'll come round the store with you after work one night and find you something really gorgeous,' she told her firmly. 'I like nothing better than telling people what they should wear,' she went on. 'Much more fun than dressing dummies in the window.' She gave Rachel an appraising look. 'With your frail, pale, gamine looks you ought to dress French.'

Rachel widened her blue eyes. 'What does that mean? Berets and striped T-shirts?'

'No, you idiot, chic and black. Something very sophisticated. Clingy. Spiky even. I know what I mean.'

'I'm not sure I do,' murmured Rachel, wondering what she had let herself in for.

'You ought to invite me to this club of yours so I can get a feel for its style,' she suggested.

Rachel shot her a grateful glance. 'I'd love you to come. I daren't mention it before because I felt so nervous, but now it would be lovely to have friends in the audience. I'll ask Ray if he'll waive the membership requirements for you. I'm sure he'll let you in as my guest.'

With everything going along so swimmingly Rachel relaxed as much as possible on the Monday. She had arranged for Lulu and her brother and a friend to come to the club on Wednesday night. But first there was 'Hilda's picnic', as everyone called the directors' luncheon.

It was being held on the upper floor in a part of the store none of them had ever been to before. Everyone was impressed by the deep blue carpet that took the place of the polished parquet of the lower levels. A glimpse through the open door of the boardroom elicited further comment. Rachel smiled. She felt quite detached from all this. Yes, it was impressive, but not overwhelmingly so. She found the formality of the occasion dull rather than daunting. Hemmed in with a plate and a drink, attended by a fleet of tail-coated waiters, she felt a sudden longing for the freedom of the open countryside. Store life, she was thinking, is a bit of a charade.

'So, do I win my bet?' A husky voice in her ear brought her back to the present with a thud. She turned and her eyes locked with a pair of laughing blue ones approximately six inches from her own. She would have liked to step back out of their electrifying range but the crush was pushing her even closer to him. She felt the hard-packed muscles skim her own body with a thrill of raw sexuality. Her face crimsoned.

The stranger from the lift was laughing softly. 'Thank heaven for crowds,' he murmured. 'It means I can get closer than I dared hope and you can't do what you would obviously like to do.'

'Which is?' she whispered furiously.

'Sink your little claws into my face by the look of it. Do you hate losing bets?'

'I didn't bet——' she began.

'What? Are you going to renege? I heard you distinctly say, "Want to bet?" when I said we'd be having lunch together. Don't tell me you've forgotten?' He pulled a face of mock hurt, looking comical and devastating at the same time.

'I hardly call this having lunch together,' she clipped.

'It wasn't exactly what I had in mind either, but it's better than nothing. I'll arrange something more to your taste next time.'

'Will you?' She gave him a haughty stare. 'You're taking rather a lot on yourself to imagine you can arrange anything for *me*.'

'Am I? Is this another brush-off?'

'What do *you* think?'

'I think you're simply playing hard to get. But you should be able to tell I'm the type who doesn't give in easily.'

His body brushed hers again and she staggered a little as she tried to step back. At once a hand shot out and he held her tightly in the small of the back. 'Very intimate,' he murmured just above her ear. 'Maybe this was a good idea after all?'

'There's no need to take the credit for yourself!' She couldn't move out of range but she could lift her chin and warn him with her eyes that she gave nought for his influence on events.

'That look,' he mocked. 'My lady Basilisk, Cruella de Ville!' He bent his head as if to glance at his watch and she felt his lips brush the side of her head.

'You're outrageous. What do you think people are going to say if they see you with your arm around me?' She felt her face flood with crimson again.

'Do you care what people say? I wouldn't have thought you gave a rap for anybody?'

'I——' She tried to think of a retort but his presence was doing the most extraordinary things to her mind. Her thoughts were scattering and skipping before her like a flock of sheep on the run. She licked her lips and tried to pull herself together. 'Is that—is that all you have to say?' she began weakly.

'Of course not.' He looked surprised. 'Now I've proved I can win, why don't you stop resisting and simply enjoy it?' He used the same husky tones as before, as if to avoid being overheard, but what it meant was that she had to strain towards him to hear what he was saying.

'You haven't proved anything,' she managed to stammer, forcing herself not to tremble as their intimacy showed no sign of ending. They seemed to be wedged between a potted palm and a chatting group from Admin, and Rachel could see no opening for escape. Besides, her limbs had turned to jelly again and seemed to refuse the command to walk away.

'Enjoy what?' she managed to ask.

'Me,' he said succinctly.

He was so blatant, it made her gasp. 'I hardly think I'll be doing *that*!' she exclaimed.

'Your eyes are the most perfect shade of cornflower I've ever seen,' he murmured, scarcely moving his lips.

'Yours are a sort of Prussian blue——' she blurted before stopping herself in confusion.

'So you have noticed?' He gave his husky laugh again. 'I knew I couldn't be wrong. Eyes like yours don't lie . . . they're wide enough to drown in.' He seemed to pull himself together. 'Tell me,' he went on conversationally, 'why do you keep trying to turn me down? What are you afraid of?' He removed his hand from the small of her back and she swayed dizzily until he ran one finger with knee-buckling slowness down the inside of her wrist towards the crease of her elbow.

Rachel felt her mouth open and close and her breath do strange jerky things in her throat before she could bring herself to speak. 'I'm not afraid of anything,' she said rapidly on one quick breath. 'I simply don't choose to get involved with strangers who try to pick me up in lifts.'

'Strangers? I don't count as a stranger, surely? I thought this company was just one big happy family?'

She couldn't help but smile, then quickly changed it to a scowl in case he thought she was weakening.

He picked up her wrist and held it between his thumb and forefinger as if taking her pulse. It was strangely soothing and arousing at the same time. 'I hope to be less of a stranger before long. That's what this is in aid of.' He glanced round the crowded room. 'Seems to be working quite well for everyone else. Why not for you?'

'I don't know why you keep trying to imply you've set something up. You haven't won your bet even if there was one because it's sheer chance we both happen to be invited to the same staff luncheon. And,' she went on, 'as I've already said, I'm not interested in getting involved with anyone. So that's that.'

'Got a boyfriend already, of course.' He frowned. 'Give him the boot. I'm the best bet.'

She smiled again. 'Honestly, you're impossible! Can't you imagine anyone turning you down because they simply don't want any involvement with anyone?'

'Does that mean no boyfriend?' He narrowed his eyes.

'Mind your own business,' she replied, nettled.

'I can find out.'

'What are you, the store detective?' She gave a little laugh. Feeling she was getting the upper hand, she said coldly, 'I'd like you to let me go, please.'

'You say that. But a few seconds ago it was a different story.'

'You took me by surprise.

He gave a little laugh and released her wrist. 'What about a pact of no involvement, then, if that's what you'd like? Play it strictly for fun?'

'Play what?'

'Us.' He eyed her expression carefully. 'I'll risk it, if you will.'

'Risk?' Now all she seemed able to do was reply in monosyllables, and he was still standing too close for comfort.

'Or are you all talk?' he was going on. 'A coward? Frightened to risk it?'

'I don't see that there's any risk,' she clipped before she could stop herself, immediately realising what she had said and what it would lay her open to.

She bit her lip as he came in at once with, 'So, if there's no risk to your freedom and your heart, Rachel Jackson, why not take a chance with me? You know it makes sense!' He was laughing now, the Prussian blue eyes full of a humour that seemed to belie the intensity of his purpose.

But Rachel was on to something else. 'My *name*!' she exclaimed. 'How on earth do you know it?' Her eyes opened very wide. '*Are* you the store detective?'

Her words sent him into a delighted chuckle. 'You should know enough to check the names of

the men who invite you to lunch,' he remarked
enigmatically, then he flicked another glance at his
watch, turning when he saw the time, saying, as the
chatting groups miraculously opened before him,
'You'll be seeing me. You can give me your answer
later!'

Senses still reeling from the encounter, Rachel
heard the sound of a voice raised above the clamour
at the upper end of the room and then Mr Maynard
was heard calling for silence. 'Ladies and
gentlemen,' he announced, holding up his hands
for quiet, and as the clink of knives and forks was
stilled he launched into a short speech of welcome
for the new director. Like everyone else she felt
herself pressing forward to see better. The dark head
of the stranger from the lift had already been
swallowed up in the crowd, she was pleased to
observe.

The half-familiar faces of the top staff were clustered near Mr Maynard, all wearing the benign
smiles of people officiating at a prizegiving. Then
they turned on cue and started to clap their hands
politely. It was then that Rachel had the shock of
her life.

CHAPTER TWO

'No!' Rachel exclaimed under her breath. Store detective? 'Oh, heavens,' she muttered, 'how could I?'

'And now,' Mr Maynard was saying with a smug smile, 'I hand you over to the newest member of our board, Mr Elliot Priest!'

Blue eyes swept the crowd, pausing only momentarily when they met her own, then turning, the smile in them unmistakable, as he addressed first his fellow directors and then the rest of the gathering.

His speech was short and humorous. Afterwards it was obvious it had endeared him to everyone. As they all filed back downstairs Rachel couldn't miss the excited chatter. Sole topic: the new director, Elliot Priest.

'Smart work, Rachel!' It was Lulu, coming into the staff-room behind her. 'I saw you both! So aren't you the dark horse? I bet he'll make you change your mind about going solo!'

'You must be *joking*!' Rachel spun to face her. 'He's the man in the lift I told you about, and precisely the sort of time-wasting womaniser I want to avoid. If you think a man like that could make me change tack, you simply don't know me at all! I don't intend to shelve my ambitions for a brief fling. And that's exactly what it would be with a man like *him*!'

In the privacy of her own thoughts Rachel had to admit that it wasn't just the disruption of a brief affair that scared her. It was more to do with the fact that she couldn't imagine a relationship that didn't mean total involvement. And that made two good reasons for keeping Elliot Priest at arm's length!

Besides, there was enough on her mind at present without wasting time even thinking about a man. Any man.

After a busy day in the store Rachel would have liked nothing better than to put her feet up for an hour or so before going out again to the club, but Ray had asked her to go in early to look over the contract he'd drawn up for her.

'At least you'll have more time to yourself when you give up your store job,' remarked Ros, noticing how tired she was looking. 'You're living on your nerves at the moment.' She herself was just on her way out to meet her boyfriend and gave Rachel a reproving look.

With the flat to herself for a while before she had to leave, Rachel pushed aside the thought that she too could be going out on a date and single-mindedly ran over some new songs until it was time to go. Constant practice had given her a large repertoire from old, sentimental ballads to the latest hits from the shows. She felt she was working towards her own individual style but wasn't sure she had found it yet.

Her first big battle was lack of confidence. It made it difficult to tell anybody about her secret dreams except for those one or two, like Ros and

Lulu, who she felt wouldn't laugh at her for being so ambitious. As the baby of a large family of brothers and sisters, all of them working in the world of farming, she had always felt too shy to confess her dreams, knowing it would lay her open to a barrage of teasing from her older brothers.

She knew they wouldn't take a career in entertainment seriously just yet, and she had enough doubts about her talent to want to cope with the doubts of those she loved. She knew she would care too much about their inevitable criticism.

When she arrived in Ray's office later on, she scanned the short contract his solicitor had drawn up. 'Do you want me to sign it now or something?' She looked round for a pen.

'No, take it home and get somebody to look it over with you. I'm not a shark, love. And I want you to be happy with it.' He gave her a fatherly pat on the shoulder. 'My own daughter's about your age. She's a dancer and she's got a nice steady boyfriend to look after her. Maybe you're the same? Talk it over together and, if you're in doubt about anything, you can always ask an independent solicitor to check it out. But——' he shook his head '—make sure we don't get into any legal wrangles. You know what these law chaps can be like and I want to keep red tape to a minimum. That's pretty standard——' He indicated the piece of paper in her hand. 'But always remember to make sure everything's watertight and don't make the mistake of getting yourself tied up for too long with anybody. You need to be free to take any opportunity that comes up if you want to get to the top.'

She agreed with this last remark emphatically, though not quite in the way Ray meant! 'I know I need to be free,' she said, and smiled.

Ray had told her he had been running clubs for years and in his heyday, as he called it, he'd run a smart club in the West End where he regularly booked top-line stars. A few years ago he had put it on the market in order to settle for somewhere less hectic in what he liked to think of as his dotage.

Rachel gave a gamine grin as she scanned the contract again. 'I'll need a manager if things really start to move, won't I?' she hinted.

But, chuckling, he shook his head. 'If I were twenty years younger, my dear, you wouldn't even have to mention it. But you need somebody young and in touch with the latest trends. I'll ask around. I still have contacts and you definitely need someone who, a, knows the ropes and b, can be trusted. A difficult combination, some might say. Really no boyfriend with your best interests at heart?'

She shook her head. 'That's the last thing I have time for.' She tilted her head pertly. 'As I've just told you, I need to be free. It's the way it has to be.'

With things moving along so well she sang with extra verve that night and finished after midnight, the audience's applause continuing long after she had returned to her dressing-room. After wearily kicking off her high-heeled shoes she removed the hairpiece Lulu had allowed her to borrow and placed it on its stand on the dressing-table. Maybe it hadn't been a good idea to wear it after all. Under the stage lights it had felt hot and uncomfortable and she couldn't stop worrying about whether it was slipping or not. It was glamorous, though, and Ray had again murmured something about wishing he was twenty years younger when he saw her in it. 'That's Zia,' he had added. 'I like her.'

She ruffled her own mouse-brown hair, easing her fingers through her scalp and resting one arm wearily on the dressing-table for a moment.

There was a knock at the door. When she called out to open it one of the waiters was revealed with a bottle of champagne and a single rose on a tray. He placed them on the dressing-table, then handed her a note. It said, 'Sorry this is such an obvious approach, but would you care to join me?' She couldn't read the signature.

'Tell him, thank you, but no.' Then she looked up. 'Should I also return the champagne?'

'That would probably be insulting,' replied the waiter evenly, then he added with a smile, 'Don't you want to know what he's like?'

'I can guess. He's about forty-five, short, fat, balding, and with a wife in the country, yes?'

'No.' The waiter shook his head. 'I'm afraid you're wrong on every count. He's also one of our best customers. I'm sure the boss wouldn't like to see him upset.'

'Are you saying I have to have a drink with him?' Suddenly she felt her spine chill. Was she getting into deep water merely by singing in a place like this? Her mother had been full of dire warnings about the wickedness of London ways. But Ray was infinitely courteous and the club, she knew from what Ros's uncle had told her, was extremely respectable. He himself was a member and had been the one to introduce her to Ray. In fact, the only wickedness she had encountered so far had been in the eminently respectable shape of Mr Priest! She let an image of his dancing blue-eyed glance float in front of her for a moment. With a little sigh she brought herself back to the present.

'I think you'd better send the whole lot back, with thanks,' she murmured. 'I would hate him to get the wrong impression.'

When the waiter left with a shrug of his shoulders, she frowned at herself in the mirror. This was where a manager would be a help. Someone, as Ray advised, who could be trusted.

She scrubbed off her make-up and put on her outdoor clothes. No doubt she could fend for herself. If not, she would have to learn.

It was with an increasing sense of effort that she managed to drag herself into work next morning. She was used to early mornings on the farm, but not late nights, and without a good eight hours behind her even store hours were difficult to keep. Knowing she was late again, she flung herself towards the lift but missed it by a hair's breadth. With an audible sigh she spun towards the stairs but was pulled up short by a muscular shape emerging from the directors' lift.

A delighted chuckle made her draw in her breath.

'So are you late or am I early?' Elliot Priest came right up to her, deliberately blocking her escape up the flight of stairs.

'Both, probably,' she muttered.

'I don't rate you for punctuality, Rachel.'

Looking at his expression she couldn't tell whether this was a formal reprimand or not. She bit her lip.

'But I certainly rate you for other, more interesting qualities,' he went on with a lowering of his voice, quenching any latent ambiguity in his words.

She drew herself up. 'As I am late, as you correctly point out, would you mind letting me past?'

'What's this, some sort of fitness routine?' he bantered, staying just where he was across the stairs. 'Why don't you use the lift?'

'It's just gone up,' she told him irritably. She would have said much more but for the knowledge now of who he was and the power he held.

'I can't have you running up five flights of stairs and arriving for work all hot and bothered,' he remarked pleasantly. Before she realised what he was doing he took her by the elbow and began to lead her towards the lift he had just stepped out of. 'Let me . . .' He held back the doors.

'I can't go in there, it's not allowed!' she exclaimed, pulling back.

'*I'm* allowing it. Do you want permission in triplicate?' His eyes still held a bantering light but Rachel got an uncomfortable feeling that their glitter could become dangerous in the batting of an eyelid.

'You do like your own way, don't you?' She hesitated, unwilling to back down.

He pushed her inside with a determined shove. 'It seems as if the only way I'm going to get anywhere with you is to throw my weight around.' The doors closed, locking them in together.

The lift seemed suddenly to shrink in size as if there were scarcely enough room for two in it. Rachel stood in the far corner and glowered. The whole thing was done out in mirrors with a deep blue carpet halfway up the walls. She could see Elliot's face in profile twice over if she turned her head. His eyes, a brighter blue than the décor, followed hers. She swung back to face him, lifting her chin, prepared for whatever challenge came her way, but unsure how to make the first defensive gestures.

'According to the maker's specifications we've got approximately thirty seconds to say what we want to say before we reach the fifth floor,' he began. 'Well?'

She glared. 'Thank you for letting me use the management's lift. It's most considerate.'

His eyes seemed luminous with laughter. 'Very cool. But it won't put me off. That's ten seconds. I'm not used to this sort of thing. Most of the women I date are people I meet socially. It's easy then. Now we're having to start from scratch. I feel like an adolescent boy, scared of putting a foot wrong. Of being turned down again. It's more scaring than hang-gliding.'

She gave a short laugh and turned away, but everywhere she looked she could see his dancing blue eyes. She closed her own eyes to shut him out.

'Don't do that,' he warned, talking rapidly all on one breath, 'you look so defenceless and I think I might have to kiss those lips to see if they're as soft as they look. And that's twenty-five seconds by the way, only five left. Rachel, have dinner with me this evening?'

She opened her eyes.

'Thirty seconds,' he said. The lift whispered to a stop. As the doors began to open he stepped in front of her. 'Well?'

She side-stepped. 'I'm late. You've already pointed that out to me.' She reached the safety of the corridor but to her alarm Elliot followed her. 'What are you doing? This isn't your floor,' she protested.

'May as well inspect the domain. Show me where you work,' he commanded.

'I'm going to get my things from the staff-room. You can't come in there!' She must have looked thoroughly horror-stricken, for he threw his head back with another of those laughs that did such strange things to her senses.

'What in heaven's name goes on that *I* can't see?' he mocked. 'Are you running an illicit gambling school or something?'

'Well,' she explained, confused, 'it's all girls. They may be changing their tights or something.'

He was chuckling again and she suddenly realised he'd been teasing her.

'You make me feel like a fool,' she mumbled, jerking away and marching off down the corridor so he couldn't see the embarrassment on her face.

'Slow down!' He caught up with her before she reached the staff-room door. 'You still haven't given me your answer.' He came right up against her and practically forced her to walk on. They reached the end of the corridor where it split off in two directions and plate-glass doors gave on to a concrete balcony. Light streamed in between the roofs of the buildings opposite and for a moment Elliot's strong, clean-cut good looks were spotlighted until he swivelled into shadow to face her. 'Well?' he prompted. 'Tonight? Or some other night? If the latter, which one?'

'For goodness' sake!' she exclaimed. 'Why are you pressurising me?'

'Because if I don't we won't get anywhere.'

She pursed her lips. 'I've told you. I can't see you.'

'Won't, you mean.'

'Can't. Won't. What difference does it make? The answer's still no.'

'You think it's no. But only because you won't admit you'd like to say yes. You would, wouldn't you?' He peered into her face.

'I doubt whether it would make much difference what I answered to that!' she came back, shooting daggers at him.

'Maybe not. Even if you were dishonest enough to say no, I'd only take it as a sign that you needed a little persuasion.'

She tried to step back, as if distance could deflect the arrowing attention aimed straight at her, but found herself up against the wall. 'No wonder you're on the board,' she muttered, trying to avoid his glance.

'What's that supposed to mean?'

'Thrusting businessman in cut-throat career,' she condemned. 'Presumably you only survive by being so domineering.'

'And being the chairman's nephew,' he added charmingly.

She suspected even he knew that had little to do with it. An attack of the swimmy feeling she had had before when he had been standing as close as he was now overcame her. She was as far back against the wall as she could be, groping for it in order to steady herself, but it didn't do any good. Why don't I just walk away? she asked herself. Because he would follow, came the prompt reply. 'I'm still saying no,' she insisted weakly.

'But it's not what you want to say.' He was looking more self-confident now for some reason.

'You must look just like this when you're winning some point at a board meeting,' she observed as acidly as she could.

He chuckled softly and moved closer. 'I hope I don't look like this at board meetings,' he said. 'It wouldn't do my reputation one iota of good if I look as starstruck as I feel.' He lifted a hand and touched her lightly on the shoulder. For a moment he was looking down at her and she up at him and they were like two figures in a tableau. Something powerful seemed to pass between them.

Rachel felt it and she knew he had felt it too. And then she had a sudden unwelcome vision of life without him. The life she had chosen, with its fame, success, the satisfaction of achieved ambitions. For an instant it all seemed somehow meaningless. She thrust the vision aside with a little gesture of annoyance.

'I really can't see you. I'm busy every evening from now until forever.'

'Doing some sort of course?' He frowned.

She glanced guiltily at the floor.

'I think you're just saying that because you're scared. I've said this before—let's play it for fun. Nothing heavy, nothing to be scared about. Let's just see each other for as long as we like it. Why ever not?'

'I've told you,' she said in a small voice, 'I don't have *time*.' The more he insisted, the more she felt she was clamming up. It was shyness again. Her crippling shyness. There was nothing to stop her explaining why she couldn't see him. The practical difficulty, that was. But then the self-defeating thought skidded into her head: who on earth do I think I am, calling myself a nightclub singer when I'm just an ordinary person? It seemed so presumptuous. If she told him he would probably roar with laughter.

She'd already battled with the thought of what Mum and Dad would say when they found out. And now she imagined the whole crowd of people back home. What, for instance, would her brothers say about quiet little Rachel growing up and trying to pass herself off as a sultry cabaret artiste? What would her Farmer's Club friends say? Her school friends? She had always longed to break out of the mould and now she was trying to do it she was overcome with self-doubts.

All it had taken was one pair of dazzling blue eyes with a casual question in them and she was back to behaving like a fourteen-year-old—'the shy one'—and if anybody at home knew they would all say, 'I told you so.' Not that they'd mean it unkindly. It was just that people liked to have other people in boxes whether the ones in the boxes wanted to be there or not.

'What's going on in that tortuous little brain of yours, Rachel?'

'Nothing,' she mumbled. She felt defeated by the complexity of her thoughts. 'Nothing's going on,' she repeated. 'I just want to get into work.'

'Oh, come on,' he said impatiently. 'What's the matter? You're interested in me. I can see that plainly enough. What's holding you back?'

Trapped against the wall and imprisoned in her own feelings too, she could only lash out at him. 'You must be one of the most arrogant men I've ever had the misfortune to encounter!' she hissed in sudden fury. 'Do you push yourself at your employees like this all the time? By what God-ordained right do you force yourself on people when they don't want you?'

He looked shocked for a moment, then, instead of allowing his own voice to rise like hers, his innate politeness took over. 'I wouldn't dream of forcing myself on you, as you put it, if you hadn't given me some hint that you rather welcomed my attentions,' he said stoically. 'You might be able to dictate the words you utter but you don't have the same control over your body language, your eyes, your——' he spread his hands '—whatever... Rachel, I'm not such an insensitive clod I can't tell you felt the same thing I felt a moment ago.'

'What thing?' she argued, truculently, bunching her hands. 'I haven't a clue what you're talking about.'

'No, of course not,' he returned sarcastically. 'Come off it, Rachel You're running scared. Don't ask me why...' He faltered as a sudden thought entered his head and his voice softened as he asked cautiously, 'You haven't been molested at some time, have you? Is that what's wrong?'

She raised her eyes heavenwards. 'You've certainly got an overheated imagination—for a *businessman*,' she added as insultingly as she could.

'That's not all that's overheated,' he rejoined half to himself, 'as you might at any moment discover!' He gazed down at her in exasperation. 'You think I'm arrogant. I think you're infuriating. Does that make us quits? Can we start from there?'

'Look, I'm already about ten minutes late——' she broke in, trying to edge out of range.

'To hell with that——' he countered.

'It's just not fair on the others,' she pointed out. 'We have to work as a team.'

He spread his hands in a gesture of surrender. 'OK. I hadn't thought of it like that.' Then he moved closer, taking her by surprise and gripping both shoulders with such sudden force that she felt her knees buckle. His lips were hovering just above her own as he glared down into her face and she noticed the slight laugh-lines on either side of his mouth. But he wasn't laughing now. His lips, full, sensual—made, she thought traitorously, for kissing—were clamped together in two firm lines and his eyes were storm-blue.

'Rachel the Rejector,' he ground out, then his fingers tightened round her shoulderbones and his lips twitched at the corners. 'I should give you a good shaking, or, better, a spanking, just to show you who's really boss,' he told her.

To forestall any such thing she retorted, 'You may be boss of the store—but you're not boss of *me*, Mr Elliot Priest——!'

'So there!' he finished for her. 'That's telling me!' He gave the warm chuckle deep in his throat that attracted her so much. 'I'm not giving in. So there to you, too! Now get along, otherwise I shall have to fire you for unpunctuality.'

'I wouldn't put it past you!' She slid out of his grasp, knees still trembling, a part of her wanting to remain in his arms even as she forced herself away, but her eyes darkened as they refused to leave his. 'If anything's said, I hope you'll be gentleman enough to explain to my supervisor why I'm so late!' she challenged.

'I'll also try to explain why you're looking so very hot and bothered, Miss Jackson,' he called after her.

'It's not on *your* account!' she sparked back untruthfully.

He came after her and the hair on the back of her neck prickled as she wondered how dangerously close he was getting. She increased her speed, and when she reached the staff-room door she couldn't help turning to see how near he was. He was almost on top of her.

Their eyes met and he gave her a high-powered smile. 'Quite a little fighter, aren't you, Miss Jackson? Better and better. I like nothing more than a good scrap!' With that he swept on towards the stairs and, contrary to his own earlier advice to her, disappeared up them three at a time.

With a sigh like a steam engine she pushed open the door. And to think the day had only just begun!

CHAPTER THREE

THE club was fuller than it had been on previous nights and, when Ray's head man showed Lulu and her two escorts to their reserved table near the front, people turned to identify the group who were getting preferential treatment. Rachel didn't linger after making sure they were all right, but went straight through to her dressing-room.

She was nervous and annoyed and not a little apprehensive. As if that morning's encounter with Elliot Priest hadn't been bad enough, Lulu had told her something else that had set her nerves jangling. Just as she was leaving the store that evening, Lulu had told her, Mr Priest had come up to her. He had asked if Rachel had already left. When Lulu said she had, he'd looked disappointed, and, feeling rather sorry for him, she had jokingly mentioned where they were going that night.

'What did he say to that?' asked Rachel, leaning forward across the table at the café where they had arranged to meet before going on to the club.

'He said——' and here Lulu gave a pussycat smile '—he wouldn't be surprised if he didn't look in himself some time.'

'*Some* time? That could mean anything. Next week even.'

'Or later tonight? At least that's how I understood him!'

45

'I hope not,' muttered Rachel crossly. The thought of those laser-bright eyes glittering at her from out of the darkness while she got herself into the mood to sing was unnerving. Then she lifted her head. 'What did he have to say about my singing there?' She couldn't imagine his reaction to that.

Lulu shrugged. 'I didn't have time to tell him. He went whizzing off at once.'

'I expect he was just saying he'd come along to be polite, the way people do,' she suggested. 'He's the nightclub type though, isn't he?'

Wondering if he would in fact turn up, she tried to take a grip on herself as she got ready to go on stage. Her self-confidence was something that came and went. Right now she was feeling small and helpless. It was partly stage fright, but the thought that Elliot Priest might be in the audience made it ten times worse.

It was with shaking fingers that she applied her make-up, then slithered into the silver tube of her dress. Then she stepped into high-heeled silver sandals and surveyed the effect in the dressing-mirror. Ray was right, she did need the hairpiece with this outfit. It was the final exotic touch.

Lifting it carefully, she placed it on her head to conceal her own pale hair. At once she was transformed into a woman of mystery. Zia seemed real, and plain Rachel existed no more. Her self-confidence rose at once. Zia was someone to hide behind. By the time she appeared in the spotlight Rachel had been relegated to a pile of street clothes in the dressing-room and Zia strutted the stage with the audience in the palm of her hand.

Afterwards she was almost too tired to go out and join her party of supporters, but politeness forced her to see that she must. Ray made an eggnog and brought it to her dressing-room. 'When are you going to give up that day job of yours?' he asked, noting her pale face now that the stage make-up had been removed.

'Soon, Ray. But I daren't burn all my bridges just yet.'

'Sensible not to give up a good, steady job. But one day you're going to have to.' He turned to go, 'By the way, you sent back a bottle of champagne last night. No need to worry, you know. I'll protect you. You can see me as a father-figure and I'd vouch for Henry any day. He's a most eligible bachelor.'

'Ray,' she half smiled, 'you *know* how I feel.'

'He's in again tonight.' Ray gave a chuckle. 'Shall I tell him no again?'

Rachel had taken the place of Zia now. She glanced at her pale peaches and cream reflection in the mirror, her hair its usual unglamorous shade of mouse, 'Does he want to see Zia?'

'Of course he does.'

'Then you'll have to tell him she's already left.'

Ray got her drift and chuckled again. 'I see what you mean. And at least he won't feel slighted. You going out to join your friends?'

She nodded, stifling a yawn. Her only hope was they wouldn't want to stay too late.

Her appearance on the other side of the foot-lights went unobserved except for one or two heads that turned to appreciate her natural beauty. She supposed she did look very different and was glad she could move about incognito. Only her own group knew she was the girl who had held centre stage no more than half an hour ago.

'You were sensational, love!' It was Lulu. The two men added their agreement. 'And I'm delighted our own little contribution helped.' She was referring to the silver wig from out of the display window. 'Tomorrow's late-night shopping. But afterwards we'll take you up to the evening-wear department and find you some more fantastic gear.'

'I can't spend too much,' Rachel murmured, weak from tiredness and the thought of having possibly to combat Lulu's over-enthusiasm.

Suddenly Lulu leaned forward and touched her on the arm. 'Look, over there by the door,' she whispered. 'He's come after all!'

Rachel peered through the haze of blue smoke to where Lulu was pointing. The figure of a man in a dinner-jacket was visible in the open doorway, the light of the foyer behind him. There was no mistaking that silhouette.

'Elliot Priest,' hissed Lulu when she saw Rachel frown. 'He said he'd come but when he didn't show up I was beginning to think you were right and he didn't mean it after all.'

'Has he just arrived?' she asked.

'Looks like it.'

Rachel felt a wave of relief. Why did it matter if Elliot Priest had witnessed her performance as the sultry, seductive Zia? She didn't know. But she knew she was relieved he hadn't seen her performance.

She soon found herself in conversation with Derek, Lulu's brother, but out of the corner of her eye she was conscious of Elliot's every move at a nearby table. He had caught sight of the group of them near the front as soon as he came in and she felt his eyes on her face as he raised his glass in a salute. Politeness forced her to respond. Later he came over.

'So did you arrive in time to hear Zia sing?' asked Lulu brightly.

'Zia? Who on earth is that? Some exotic snake-dancer?' he quipped.

'Well, actually——' she continued.

'Just a third-rate cabaret singer,' broke in Rachel bitingly. 'Hardly your cup of tea I would have thought, Mr Priest.' She flashed a warning glance around the surprised group then turned a challenging look on Elliot.

'I must admit my taste runs to opera rather than cabaret,' he agreed looking straight at her. 'So how about a dance?'

'That doesn't follow,' she began weakly, but he was standing beside her chair and without creating a scene she had no option but to accept the hand he held out.

What she wanted to say to him once they were out of earshot was already prepared in her mind, but the instant his body touched her own she felt hopelessly tongue-tied. It was as if he sapped her will just by looking at her.

'Still fighting me?' he murmured in her ear. 'Why bother? This is heaven, isn't it? We two and the night and the music.'

'You sound like a bad novel!' she exclaimed.

'When emotion runs high, cliché comes into its own. Like a patient waking up in hospital and uttering the immortal words, "Where am I?" The point isn't whether it's cliché but whether it's genuine.'

'I thought we were supposed to be dancing?'

His hands ran up then down, covering her spine in a warm glow. 'Is that what you call it? It seems more like making love.'

'Elliot, stop it.' She tried to draw back.

'I can't.'

'You're not trying!'

'I know. I'd rather go on doing this forever—and maybe one or two other things as well. Like me to show you what I mean later?'

'You're playing with me!' The Rachel side of her, the girl with little confidence, was longing to ask him what he imagined he was doing making a play for a girl like her, when, as nephew of the chairman, he must be used to any number of spoilt little rich girls who knew their way around and would be able to field his advances, or not, with much more expertise than she could. 'I'm not your type,' she blurted.

'What is my type?' He pressed his lips against the side of her head.

'Girls who have everything,' she said firmly, 'and can handle men like you!'

'Wrong,' he smiled, lifting his lips and looking down at her with a smile that sent warning shivers down her back. '*You're* my type, Rachel Jackson— sweet, innocent Rachel!'

She was silent. And after a long pause he said, 'And I'm not playing with you. I suspect you simply haven't met many men like me.'

The smoochy number they were swaying to ended just then and the trio struck up with a medley of rock 'n' roll oldies. Elliot led her to the side of the floor.

'I'd like to talk to you but the decibel level is a little high. Any suggestions as to what we might do?'

She shook her head, glancing across to where Lulu and her boyfriend were sitting.

'Your escort seems to have found another partner,' he informed her, observing the direction of her glance, 'Are you bothered?'

'Of course not. He's Lulu's brother and this is the first time we've met——' She broke off when she saw the smile of satisfaction on Elliot's face.

'Good,' he replied succinctly. 'I wouldn't like a fight on my hands.' And before she could comment he went on, 'Let's meet as soon as we can tomorrow. Where do you usually have lunch?'

She was lip-reading. Lost in the tiny movements that allowed words to form as if they were weaving some enchantment over her. 'Sorry?' she asked, leaning closer, her eyes still on his lips.

'That's better.' He looped his arms around her waist. 'Stay close. Let's not bother to talk.'

'But what did you say?' she asked, trying to still the dizzying sensation of his touch beneath an air of practicality.

'I asked where you usually had lunch.'

'Oh.' She paused. 'In the staff rest-room, of course.'

'Sandwiches in the staff rest-room,' he breathed. 'Wonderful. I wish I could join you——'

'Elliot, *no*!'

He laughed aloud at the horrified look she gave him. 'Then meet me somewhere else. Somewhere,' he added, 'where you won't be ashamed to be seen with me.'

'Hardly ashamed,' she corrected. 'I just don't want to become a subject of gossip.' She averted her head.

'Tomorrow, then.' He pressed his lips against the side of her hair, taking advantage of the darkness, as the house lights went down and the resident comic took the stage, to press a burning kiss against the side of her mouth.

Rachel pretended to be interested in the rather way-out jokes that had the rest of the audience in stitches, but all she really wanted to do was escape. The magic spell of Elliot's touch had bound her thoughts so tightly she couldn't work out what was happening to her. She had never felt such wild emotions before. They didn't make sense.

Crawling home at three in the morning, she was very glad Ros hadn't been at the club. By now she would have been pointing out how attractive Elliot was and how, in her own view, 'people need people', and she would have blown the whole thing up into a 'serious relationship'—something it could never be. Elliot was a flirt, out for a good time, and for some obscure reason best known to himself he seemed to imagine he could have one with her! Well, he would soon get a rude awakening, for an affair with such a heart-breaker was the last thing she intended.

She slid into bed. She had agreed to a lunch date. Nothing more.

*   *   *

The morning dragged. She redressed one of the windows three times. It wouldn't go right. The models were supposed to look graceful, elegant, full of respose. Instead two of them seemed to be involved in some particularly angry argument while the third looked on with an expression of detached scorn.

'They won't sell clothes looking like that,' she said to Lulu when she came down with the accessories.

'Something on your mind?'

'Why should there be?'

'Just looking at what you've made the models do.'

'I haven't *made* them do it. They just seem to go that way.'

'It's your unconscious coming to the surface. Conflicts, conflicts. I read a book about it. It's like children playing with dolls to get rid of deep-seated emotional problems.'

'You're very clever this morning, Lu.'

'It's from spending the evening with my brother. He brings it out in me like a rash. Where do you want this gear? I can't put it out yet if you're going to change their positions.' She dumped it in a corner of the window. 'Let me know when you're ready and I'll come back.'

Rachel struggled on but the final result seemed little better. She wondered if Lulu was right. But she had no problems, emotional or otherwise. Her life couldn't be more straightforward. Even as she sat eating her sandwiches in the staff rest-room as usual she could tell herself quite confidently that she had no problems at all.

'Coffee, anyone?' It was one of the girls from Haberdashery.

'I'll do it.' Rachel got up. She was feeling restless. Anything was better than just sitting. 'I must be overworking,' she said to no one in particular. 'I can't concentrate.' She knocked over a pile of mugs, breaking one. He had said lunch. *Now* it was twenty to two. She'd been right about him all along.

She poured boiling water into six mugs and started to hand them round when one of the juniors from the perfume counter came in. 'There you are, Rachel. There's a message for you to go up to heaven.'

'Heaven?' By that the girl meant the seventh floor. Rachel went hot and cold all over. But the girl's next words were like a cold douche.

'It was from Hilda's secretary,' she added.

'What's old Hilda want with you?' Lulu puzzled.

'Probably about that window this morning,' muttered Rachel, reddening as she realised that this was more likely than the wayward thought that had instantly and shamingly careered through her head. Of *course* he'd been playing games, despite his denial. He'd had no intention of inviting a mere employee to lunch. He had probably just wanted to see what she'd say. She swallowed her coffee and went out.

The lift brought her smoothly to the seventh floor and she stepped out on to the deep blue carpet like a swimmer setting out across a strange sea. But she had only reached the halfway point when she felt a hand on her elbow. She spun round straight into Elliot's arms.

'If you've already eaten I shall be furious.'

She drew back. 'Of *course* I've eaten,' she exclaimed. 'It is nearly two o'clock.'

'Eat again, with me,' he suggested.

'I've just had a message to go and see Hil—I mean Mr Maynard,' she told him primly.

'That was from me, you idiot. Come along.' He began to pull her along towards one of the many doors that lined the corridor. 'I got stuck in some board meeting and couldn't get out,' he told her airily. 'I didn't think you'd mind as we hadn't bothered to arrange a specific time.'

'Couldn't you have sent a message out?'

Ignoring her protests, he led her to a table set with a white cloth on a balcony. Over the edge of the ornamental sandstone balustrade she could see the roofs of London.

She stood beside the table, still annoyed that he had taken her for granted. Then she bit her lip. What a stupid thing to think! What would the other directors say if they knew he was actually dating one of the staff, an underling? She turned miserably to the balcony and pretended to be looking for landmarks among the turrets and towers.

He came to stand behind her. 'I should have done that. You're right.' She felt a kiss on the nape of her neck. 'At least have a glass of wine and some cake.' He moved away. 'Or would you prefer coffee? Or what about some ice-cream or a piece of this rather splendid gâteau?' He was scanning the table for inspiration.

'I don't want anything,' she began, then added, 'but you must eat.'

'I'm going to. And I'm going to open a bottle of wine and if we don't finish it now you must come back after work and—Rachel, why do we never have the time to sit and talk like other people? I have an appointment with the money-men at three.' He flicked a glance at his watch. 'Here.' He uncorked the bottle and poured her a glass.

She toyed with it without lifting it to her lips. 'I should be back at work now.'

'A few minutes. Otherwise I'll have to eat alone.'

'Is that so bad?' She couldn't help giving a grudging smile.

'Disastrous.'

'Elliot——' She paused. 'This can't work, can it?'

'What?' He was tucking into a large hunk of quiche, thus contradicting the adage, for there was nothing unreal about his masculinity... She brought her mind back to the present.

'Us, seeing each other, I mean.'

'Why the hell not? *You* want to. *I* want to. Now stop going back over old ground. We've done this one. You pretending not to be interested, while your eyes, your—everything——' he waved a hand vaguely '—tells another story.'

'I'm not going over old ground. This is an objection I hadn't thought of before.' She didn't know why she didn't confess the real objection. But just now this one seemed real enough.

'Unecessary.'

'What is?'

'To keep thinking of objections. You should realise by now I shall simply sweep them all away. Whatever they are,' he added darkly.

'I don't think you can sweep this one away. I'm an employee. And you——'

'Yes?' he prompted.

'You're the boss's nephew, for heaven's sake! We're worlds apart.'

'Rubbish.'

She drew herself up. 'You're in charge, Elliot. It feels wrong.'

'I'm in charge, true. So that bothers you, does it? Don't you realise I'd be in charge anyway, even if I were a news-seller? You'll get used to it. I'm very easygoing when you get to know me.'

'Oh, yes?' She gave him a scathing glance. The phrase 'life in the fast lane' might have been invented for him, and he was certainly the type to call the shots, no matter what situation he was in.

'I still don't think there's any point,' she persisted.

'You'll adapt. I bet you're a really fast learner. Look how well you've adapted to city life after only three months. Your trouble is, you have no faith in yourself.'

She lifted her head. It was so accurate an assessment of what she knew was the truth that she couldn't think of anything to say. How could he read her so well? After a long pause she said, 'Am I so transparent?'

'I'm afraid you are.' He chuckled. 'That's what I adore about you. It makes such a change from the usual lacquered female one finds in town. What part of the country are you from anyway?'

She was still coming to terms with what he had just said about adoring her until he prompted, 'You're not a Londoner. I can tell that much.'

'No.' She avoided his glance. 'Actually I'm from Dorset. Dad's a farmer.'

'That accounts for your milkmaid look!' He reached out and placed one hand over one of hers where it rested on the balustrade. Neither of them spoke. Rachel was conscious of the warmth of his skin. It was a protective sort of touch, making her feel she could trust him. But, she thought with a sudden shudder, it was based on a mistake. She wasn't the girl he thought she was. Obviously he saw her sitting at home in the evenings with her embroidery. *Milkmaid*? It brought an image of rustic innocence to mind. Early nights and apple cheeks. Purity and prettiness.

What would he think if he knew she was a nightclub singer? About to tell him, she was stalled when he gave another impatient glance at his watch. 'I'll have to go. Drink up your wine and come straight up at six o'clock.'

He was halfway to the door.

'Elliot, I *can't*.'

He frowned. 'Will you please stop saying that?'

'But it's fact. Surely you can't have forgotten it's late-night closing tonight?'

He banged a fist against his forehead. 'Eight, then?'

She shook her head. 'I've agreed to meet some friends.'

He put on a pained expression. 'Look, we're going to meet. I'll contact you during the afternoon.'

The afternoon, she thought, looking down at the lunch table, is more than half over already.

CHAPTER FOUR

THE plate-glass windows effectively shut out the sound of the Piccadilly-bound traffic in the street outside, and Rachel always felt she was in a world of her own when putting a display together, even though she was always aware of the many passers-by who stopped to stare.

As she scattered handfuls of white daisies over the display, the final touch in the romantic little scene she had created to show off some garden party dresses, she became conscious of somebody peering in to watch. Usually people walked on after a few seconds but this one stayed. Eventually she glanced up. Afterwards she was glad she was kneeling down at the foot of one of the models or she might have stumbled. As it was she did a double-take and nearly dropped the basket of daisies crooked under one arm.

It was Elliot, grinning in at her like an idiot. He mouthed something but she couldn't tell what he was saying, so she turned back to scattering the daisies, furious with herself for the blush she felt spread its incriminating rose colour over her exposed skin.

When she dared look up again he was standing talking to two other businessmen beside a limousine. They must have been the money-men he mentioned. He looked impossibly rakish compared to the rather staid, paunchy grey-haired appearance of the other two. Even his dark business suit emphasised his lethal attractiveness, suggesting something animal forced tightly under control.

She turned back, determined not to be caught watching him. When she finished off, locking the door to the window behind her, he had already gone.

'In the window among the daisies—we should make you a permanent feature. Sales would rocket.' His husky voice stopped her with her hand on the lift button. She jerked round as the doors slid open.

'Come on.' Pushing her on ahead, he stepped in just as someone made a dash across the foyer to get in with them. He closed the door before they were even halfway across.

'You shouldn't have done that,' she began, but he was smiling down at her, one hand resting on the wall above her head, making the words die in her throat. Without letting his glance leave her face, he reached out and picked up one of the few remaining daisies in the basket and placed it gently in her hair.

'You're so sweet.' His voice was throbbing with obvious emotion, the bantering smile deserting his eyes and being replaced by something more predatory as he began to lower his head.

Pressing herself back against the side of the lift, Rachel muttered a weak, 'No, Elliot——' as it was all too obvious what he intended, but the rest of what she wanted to say was stopped by the gentle pressure of his lips on hers. Suddenly she found herself wrapped in his arms, their bodies melding in a feverish collision of desire that sent all thought of resistance flying away. His hot tongue probed the softness between her lips, demanding a response she couldn't deny him. In her confusion she thought fire was engulfing her melting limbs and she brought up one hand for help, finding that instead her fingers ran helplessly of their own accord through the thick dark hair at the back of his head.

The lift came to an abrupt stop and as the doors began to slide back he released her. He was breathing heavily. In a dream she saw his hand reach out towards the push-button, but she put out her own hand.

'No, please, Elliot, please don't do this—I——' She broke off, not sure what to say. She wanted and she didn't want. She was poised on the crest of a wave and felt she might crash down to destruction—or be engulfed in a sublime joy. Her knees were trembling as if to express the fear that suddenly shook through her.

He was somehow standing next to her in the corridor while people pushed and shoved past them into the lift. Rachel was scarcely conscious of anything but her resistance to what it was she feared from him. It surfaced, taking hold of her mind.

'Let me go,' she said in a high, tight voice. She brushed his detaining hand away from her shoulder.

He mistook her tone and her gesture for anger. 'Don't say you didn't want it too!' he rapped, suddenly losing control. His eyes blazed like blue flame.

'Go away, I said!' She glanced from side to side but there was nobody within earshot. Fear made her turn on him. She could see the destruction of all her ambitions, just looking at him. It was like reading the future in his eyes. She knew intuitively that she was laying herself open to the danger of relinquishing worlds for him. He was that sort of man, and he was right when he said she had never met anyone like him—she had never met any man who could make her imagination and her emotions whip into such a storm merely in response to his touch. What was needed now was coolness, objectivity.

She drew her shaking body together with an effort. 'Don't do that again, Mr Priest, even if you *are* the chairman's nephew,' she said as cuttingly as she could.

'I'll wait for you after you finish tonight,' he rapped out, ignoring her words and turning away.

'Don't bother! I'm meeting friends!' she called after him. He neither replied nor turned to acknowledge her rejection.

'This one! And the black. You simply must take the black, Rachel!' Lulu held up a skimpy frock the price of which seemed to be in inverse proportion to the amount of material used.

'But what about the scarlet taffeta?' It was the fashion assistant who was helping them. Rachel herself frowned.

'I still don't feel any of them are right.'

'But how do you see yourself?'

'Myself?' Rachel gazed at her image in the mirror. She saw Rachel now, that was the trouble. She saw a girl with an armful of white daisies. A milkmaid. Roses and cream. Spring idyll. Innocence. But what she needed to see, what she wanted to see, was tough, ambitious Zia, the woman with the world at her feet. Or at least, with a successful career as a singer ahead of her.

She turned. 'I feel confused,' she confessed. 'On stage I have to put on an act. To be Zia. On stage it's so easy. She seems more real than real. But off stage—I don't know. I can't grasp her somehow. I just don't know what she would look like any more.'

'We're here to help, love. And I see Zia as very sultry, very womanly.' Lulu turned to the assistant. 'Know what I mean? Somebody rather wicked, a sort of *femme fatale*.'

'Heavens!' murmured Rachel faintly.

'But you must admit, Rachel, that's how you put your songs over. I mean, it's so right. That's what the songs are really saying. You can't sing about temptation and look like a schoolgirl——' She paused. 'Well, maybe you could.' She was off on another tack and rummaged among the racks for something in white but Rachel shook her head.

'Maybe I simply need more time to get into the part. There's no urgency about this. Ray seems happy with the way I look. The audience like it. It's just—well,' she shrugged, 'I never expected to have to act to this extent. At first I thought it was just a case of getting out there and singing to my very best. But the audience seems to change things and somehow I found myself acting for them, to them . . . and you're right. I have to dress the part if I'm singing about love.'

'There might be a sort of piquancy about innocence and temptation,' mused Lulu. 'Think of Doris Day.'

'I am *not* going out there in a Peter Pan collar!' Rachel grinned suddenly. 'You two are sweet to try to help me. Shall we leave it for now and see if we can come up with something some other time?'

Reluctantly Lulu replaced the black dress on its hanger. 'If you're not having this one I might break the bank and get it for myself. With the staff discount I might just be able to afford it.'

'Is your boyfriend the man to appreciate that sort of thing?' remarked the assistant wickedly.

Lulu pulled a face. 'No, but I know who is!' She gave a sidelong glance at Rachel. 'Don't you agree?'

Rachel, still in bra and panties, pulled her sweater roughly over her head and used it as a hiding-place to conceal her reaction. When she emerged she managed to say flippantly, 'I can't imagine who on earth you mean.'

She had tried to squash any speculation about what was going on between her and Elliot, but Lulu's curiosity wasn't easily put to rest and she gave her a knowing smile.

A few minutes later they thanked the senior sales girl who had stayed behind to help them, then got their coats from the cloakroom and descended to the ground floor. It was nearly nine o'clock. The two of them stood in the entrance for a moment.

'Home to supper,' said Lulu, 'and an early night. What about you?'

'I think I'll have to go straight on to the club,' said Rachel. 'It's too late to go home.' Already her stage fright was coming back. She turned, too nervous to stand and chat. Lulu followed her out on to the pavement.

A white convertible was parked on the double yellow lines, its roof partly back and the sounds of music, an aria from some opera, clearly floating into the night air. Rachel stopped dead.

'It's him,' whispered Lulu. 'And he's coming over.'

She was right. Elliot must have been watching from the car, for as soon as the girls appeared he climbed out and came round its bonnet towards them.

'I've got to go——' Rachel said wildly. At that moment a taxi cruised into sight. With a gasp she ran towards it, her arm outstretched. Thankfully it swooped towards the kerb at once.

'The Manhattan Club near Bond Street,' she said rapidly, scrabbling at the nearside door and throwing herself thankfully on to the back seat as she heard Elliot's shout behind her. The driver put his foot down and tried to edge back into the stream of traffic, but there was a delay and it was enough for Elliot to wrench open the door and throw himself into the back beside her.

'Elliot, *no!*' She turned on him, blue eyes blazing at his effrontery.

'You *saw* me waiting for you,' he rasped, 'so why did you run off like that?'

'I told you—it's no good. I'm—I'm busy tonight anyway.'

'Busy? Meeting some chap at the Manhattan?' Obviously he had picked up on her instructions to the cab driver. 'You weren't there with anyone special last night, so you said. Or are you seeing that brother of Lulu's again?' He gave a derisive smile. 'If that's the case I'd better come with you as protection.'

'What about your car?' she said, clutching at straws.

'Damn!' He scowled, obviously having forgotten all about it. 'I've warded off one set of traffic wardens, plus I've left the keys in the ignition. *Are* you meeting someone, Rachel?' he demanded, looking her square in the face.

She shook her head, unable to lie to him.

He waited long enough to catch her reply, then he tapped on the window to ask the taxi driver to set him down. 'I'll see you there.'

'No, Elliot!' But her cry was in vain. He leaped from the cab and started back towards his own car.

Now what am I to do? she asked herself angrily. Contradictions raged in her head. He would see clearly she wasn't the milkmaid type of his imagination when he witnessed her act. But did that matter? She didn't want an entanglement with him because she knew that for him it could never be serious. As he'd said at the beginning, he wanted to play it for fun. She just happened to be a girl who had caught his eye and obviously her resistance to him had had the opposite effect intended, inflaming his ardour instead of cooling it.

If she had known him at the beginning she would have guessed that he was the type to enjoy the challenge of pursuit, but it was too late to change all that now. On top of all that she had to be single-minded about her career if she wanted to get anywhere. That was the vow she had made to herself. So why did she care that he might get the wrong impression?

I *don't* care, she told herself fiercely. All I care about is my career. Elliot Priest can keep away!

She fully expected to see the white convertible pull in behind the cab when she alighted a few minutes later in a lane off Bond Street, but there was no sign of it and she wondered if he had perhaps taken heed of her vehement response to his overture. Thankful for this slight reprieve, she hurried into the club and made straight for her dressing-room to prepare herself. In all the confusion she had quite forgotten she was supposed to be suffering stage fright. She smiled grimly into the mirror. At least Elliot's importuning had had some positive effect!

The place was crowded when she finally stood in the spotlight. She couldn't make out the faces in the audience, but she could feel the warmth and excitement of the crowd pressing round in the darkness beyond the rim of light. Ray had already told her there was a full house. He was turning people away, he told her. She was beginning to be hot news. There was obviously something else he wanted to say but instead he simply patted her on the shoulder as she listened to the first bars of her tune, and with a little smile went out to announce her. The applause was electric. Rachel ceased to exist and Zia, smiling and full of confidence, stepped into the light.

Afterwards her room was an island in a sea of compliments. Even with the door closed she could hear the applause beating relentlessly in the distance. Ray knocked, then poked his head round. 'No, I'm not going to ask you to drag yourself out there again, sweetheart. You've given them four encores. They'll have to come back if they want more. But there is someone here to see you. Do you mind?'

Zia—she still wore the silver wig and one silver sandal was swinging from the ends of her toes as she sat on the stool in front of her lighted dressing-mirror—pivoted. Ray's words had made her heart lurch, but it was followed at once by a sigh of relief. A tall, slightly stoop-shouldered man with a moustache and immaculately tidy brown hair came through the doorway.

He held out a hand. 'Zia, so kind to see me. I'm Herman Ward.' He obviously expected his name to mean something and her quick glance of appeal to Ray showed that he had hoped to forearm her before her privacy could be invaded. Behind the stranger's back he spread his arms helplessly then moved forward.

'Herman is an agent with Southern Artists. He was very interested in your performance tonight.'

'Very interested indeed, my dear.' Herman, having shaken her by the hand, still held it in his.

She withdrew it carefully and moved back. Rachel might have blushed. But Zia drew herself up. 'You're too kind.' She gave him a limpid smile. Herman turned to Ray as if expecting him to leave but Zia fixed him a look of appeal again and, reading it, he remained staunchly where he was. 'May I offer you a drink before you go home, Zia?' he murmured. 'I know you always want to get away as soon as you finish.'

'Family commitments?' asked the smooth Mr Ward.

'No.' Zia smiled but, enigmatically, failed to en-large on why she always left straight away.

The purpose of Herman Ward's visit, she soon discovered, was to discuss the likelihood of her compatibility with the agency, as he put it.

After he had courteously cut short his stay in deference to her wish to leave early, she mused over these words as the wig and the silver dress, the sandals and the diamanté earrings were stowed away for the night. What about the compatibility of the agency with *me*? she wondered. That, she thought a little crossly, was important too.

'Changed your mind, did you?' It was raining in sharp, nasty gusts and the garden party window display looked rather forlorn. Elliot, in a full-length Burberry, its collar pulled right up, half obscuring his face, caught Rachel by the elbow as she hurried towards the staff entrance. He guided her roughly back into the street and proceeded to hurry her along the expanse of window space that fronted Knightsbridge.

'It's eight-fifty in the morning——' she knew to the minute because of a delay on the Tube making her think she'd be late '—and *I* have to clock on even if *you* don't.'

'I asked you a question.'

'I heard you.'

'I want an answer, Rachel.' His blue eyes were expressionless. 'Out of curiosity,' he amended, 'just where *did* you go last night? I followed as quickly as I could but you seemed to vanish into thin air. Did I make you change your plans? Are you *so* anxious to avoid seeing me?'

She walked on rapidly, aimlessly, head high, rain plastering her hair to her forehead. When she came to the end of the block she stopped abruptly. 'Look, I really do have to go into work.'

'You're not going anywhere until I have a satisfactory answer,' His grip tightened on her elbow. 'Now come on, you can be back inside in two seconds flat if you co-operate.'

'I went to the club. Of course I did. I——' she bit her lip, choosing her words carefully '—I didn't see you there.'

'I was there. I had to sit through the cabaret. I thought when the lights came up I would see you at the next table or something.' His face darkened. 'For God's sake, Rachel. Don't thwart me. It's nonsense. Why are you doing it?'

His grip tightened and she made a sudden effort to wrestle free but he merely increased the pressure and she saw from his expression that he wasn't going to let her go. A tide of anger swept through her. 'Don't *I* have any choice in this?' she said with venom, keeping her voice low so as not to attract the attention of the passers-by. 'Surely it's enough if I say I don't *want* to see you? What have my reasons got to do with *you*? Who *are* you? God Almighty?'

Instead of rounding on her, he released her arm so suddenly that she nearly fell. He caught her again. Putting both arms tightly round her and holding her against him in a sort of embrace, his lips scarcely moving, he said, 'I'm not God Almighty and I'm not the store detective either. Though I damn well wish I had been last night. Maybe then I would have been able to find out where you disappeared to. Come on. Let's go back. You're getting wet.'

He looped his arm around her waist and forced her to walk back alongside him until they came to the staff door again. 'Am I supposed to accept defeat?' He sounded bemused and there was a glint in his eyes that was no longer due to anger. 'I'm not used to being turned down. Perhaps I'll go back to the Manhattan,' he mused, eyes bright. 'That singer they've got there was really something. Maybe *she*'d appreciate what I've got to offer! In fact after her performance last night,' he gave a short laugh, 'I'm sure she would!'

'What *do* you mean?' She gave him a sidelong glance.

He began to chuckle. 'You'd have to be a man to understand a woman like that. I won't shock your innocent little ears by trying to explain. Suffice it to say, I think my poor battered ego——' he gave another chuckle '——would receive the attention it deserves in the arms of the fabulous Zia!'

'I wouldn't be too sure about *that*.' Rachel scowled up at him.

'Are you challenging me again, Rachel?'

'What do you mean?'

'You don't think much of me, do you? Do you really think *she'd* turn me down too?'

'Yes,' she said shortly, swivelling into the entrance. He pulled her back.

'Want to bet?'

'I don't bet.'

'No, but you sure believe in throwing down the gauntlet. Tell me something.' He put an arm confidentially around her shoulders and drew her to one side so that they were unobserved. 'Are you still playing games or are you definitely saying no to me?'

She nodded, painfully aware of the virile strength of him, the sharp, arousing scent of his skin numbing her resistance. 'I'm saying no,' she replied slowly.

Swiftly his lips were on hers and her own traitorous response quickened her pulses and made her mouth open softly to receive his assault, but before she could register what was happening he drew back. His lips twisted with derision. ' "No," she says. "No." I've never met a woman who could say no the way you do! But so be it. You realise, of course, that you leave me no option?' He released her, letting his hands drop roughly away so that she felt as if something had ripped them both asunder.

'No option,' he went on, 'but to seek solace in the arms of the amazing Zia!' He gave a hard laugh.

Rachel could only stand and watch as he crossed the foyer to the directors' lift. He got in as she went on staring after him and then the doors drew together so that the last thing she saw was the jut of his chin and his expression as his eyes challenged her own.

CHAPTER FIVE

SUCH had been Elliot's mood when they parted that Rachel fully expected him to try to fulfil his intention to seek solace in the arms of Zia at once—if he could manage it! But after her performance, not sure whether he had even been in or not, she saw no sign of him. There was, however, the usual bottle of champagne and a single long-stemmed rose from her faithful admirer referred to by Ray as 'long-suffering Henry' and there were more in an increasing number of invitations, both written and verbal, from other members of the audience.

Rachel didn't like it much, but she didn't see what she could do about it—except to keep on saying no.

She was now firmly established as resident *chanteuse*, as Ray suddenly decided to call her, and she wondered what she might have to do to instigate her next career move. One possibility was to accept an invitation to meet Herman Ward in order to discuss representation by Southern Artists.

She gave the matter careful consideration. And finally, though she decided to be prudent and decline his offer of dinner *à deux*, she did agree to have lunch with him, the proviso being that as she was a working girl he would have to meet her at work, in the garden restaurant at the store.

Herman Ward turned up on time, his hair, as before, so immaculately in place that she suspected

it might be a toupée. He was businesslike but did
not try to conceal his personal interest in her either.

'It's quite a surprise to see the fabulous
Zia——' it seemed to have become a catch-phrase,
she noted '—in the cold light of day. Nothing like
lunch to deglamorise a myth,' he added, rather
cynically. Then, as if to counter any sense of criticism in the remark, he added, 'I'm not sure which
one of you I prefer. You're really a very beautiful
young woman, my dear. It will be a privilege to
represent you.' He bowed his head courteously.
Rachel was finally convinced it was a toupée and
silently observed that she and Herman had one
thing in common at least.

Today her mousy hair had been highlighted in
the store salon and piled on top of her head in what
she hoped was a style of smooth sophistication. Her
salary had stretched to a neat dark suit with a short
skirt that showed off her perfect legs and she hoped
she looked businesslike and, with the silk shirt
fastened at the neck by a borrowed gold clip, coolly
glamorous.

Herman was obviously much taken with this new
image and couldn't take his eyes off her. But, when
it came to the terms of the contract his agency
wanted to offer her, he became sharp enough to
make her realise she was getting out of her depth.
He seemed to want an awful lot of power over her
future. He promised to send a copy of their
standard contract so that she and her manager—
he paused—could look it over. She didn't like to
tell him that she was her own manager, thinking it
might be safer if he thought she had some tough-
minded protector in the background.

'We'll read it over and think about it,' she told him.

They concluded lunch with glasses of brandy and Rachel's glance at the time eventually brought the meeting to an end. Herman walked to the entrance with her after settling the bill and took one of her hands in his. Kissing the back of it, he murmured, 'Here's to the next time. May it be soon, my dear.'

As she watched him leave she felt someone brush against her and, thinking it was a customer wanting to leave the restaurant, she stepped to one side. Then she found herself being glowered at by an obviously irate Elliot.

'A little old and—how shall we say?——' he paused with delicate irony '—well *used* for someone of your age, isn't he, Rachel?'

Her mouth opened and closed. It seemed an age since she had seen him. He was wearing a light-coloured summer suit that accentuated his hint of a tan. His hair was glossy, very black and infinitely touchable. Only his expression, the arctic sweep of those scornful blue eyes, warned her to check any show of the wild longing his appearance aroused.

'He's——' she swallowed to regain control of a voice that came out like a croak '—he's a very nice man.'

Elliot's face was a picture of disdain. 'No accounting for taste, is there? But obviously you have lots in common, judging by the way you were hanging on his every word.' Plainly he couldn't accept what he mistakenly believed to be true. She wanted to tell him he was wrong to make assumptions, but his anger seemed to annihilate the impulse to speak. Without waiting for a reply he swept

on, punching the lift button to carry him to the
seventh floor, his handsome features covered in a
scowl.

That night she wore the little black nothing of a
dress Lulu had picked out, and with black spiky
heels, black stockings and a short wig that was just
a neat cap of party glitter she felt chic and, as Ray
said when he saw her in the corridor, utterly sinful.
He gave her an avuncular pat on the shoulder before
she went on.

She had decided to try out a few standards for
a change, like 'Smoke Gets in Your Eyes',
'September Song', 'If I Loved You', taking a short
break in the middle, then afterwards, in a frou-frou
outfit of red taffeta and black net, bouncing back
with a series of more upbeat numbers. When it was
over she asked Ray if she should have performed
them the other way round—sad songs second. He
smiled contentedly.

'Zia, perform them back to front or upside-down
if you like. Whatever you do is spot-on.'

If that were only true, she thought with a stab
of pain as she recalled Elliot's words that afternoon. Ray brought her a hot drink, knowing by
now that she wouldn't touch alcohol. 'There's
something for you in my office. It wouldn't fit in
here.' He glanced round the cramped dressing-
room. Puzzled, she followed him down the corridor. An enormous basket of flowers stood in pride
of place on his desk.

'Heavens!' She gulped at the sight. The room was
filled with their exotic perfume.

'For you.'

'Why thank you, Ray, I——'

'Not from me, child. From one of your many admirers.' He chuckled. 'Long-suffering Henry seems to have a rival.'

She approached the display and looked for a card. There wasn't one. 'Heavens,' she said again. The tropical colours glowed under the office strip-light, only their delicate shapes balancing what might have been an overpowering gaudiness.

She bent to smell a single white bloom, basking for a moment in the heady perfume that enveloped her. Tears came into her eyes. Not from the scent but from emotion, a knot of it, welling up unbidden inside her. If only this were a gift from Elliot, she thought, she would cherish every last petal. But she had put paid to any relationship with him for good and all now. She dashed away the silver drops and jerked her head up to look at Ray.

'Singing those nostalgic old songs has really taken it out of me,' she muttered, trying to avoid his eye. 'I feel sort of shaky.' It was ridiculous. She couldn't understand what had got into her. Things were going so well.

'Take it easy, kiddo. You had half the audience in tears too. I think, in answer to your former question, you'd better stick to the current sequence otherwise we're going to have them going home with their faces buried in their hankies!' He patted her shoulder. 'Want me to try to find out who sent them?'

She shook her head. 'It wouldn't matter anyway. If he wanted thanks he'd have left a name.'

'I'll help you get them out to a cab.' He reached for the phone.

'I'll change. Ask the cab to come round straight away, would you?' She went back to the dressing-room and removed her make-up and the false eyelashes she had been experimenting with. Men were strange, she thought. Would they send flowers if they saw her now, pale-faced and without the make-up? Yet she was still the same girl, despite the lack of glitz and glam. Feeling disturbed by the effect of something as artificial as mere appearance on her audience, she slipped thoughtfully into her street clothes. Elliot Priest, too, had fallen for an illusion if he seriously saw her as nothing more than an apple-cheeked country girl.

Ray eventually came staggering down the corridor with the flowers. She held the door then followed him out. The cab driver didn't bat an eye at his extra 'passenger'. She had to carry it up the steps to her flat herself when they arrived. Everything seemed like a dream, she felt, at one remove from reality. Somehow she had never felt so alone in her entire life.

Lulu was looking gloomy, and she continued, 'You're a good window-dresser, Rachel. I shall be sorry to lose you.'

Rachel had just broken the expected news that she was going to hand in her notice. 'In another four weeks,' she explained. 'I may be under contract to Southern Artists and the bookings should be starting to come in. I'll need the daytime to rehearse new songs and get myself organised.' Though she spoke cheerfully enough, there was a strange heaviness in her heart. She put it down to the fact that she was leaving one phase of her life behind, and the future, like anything unknown, seemed a little scary. Besides, she'd been happy enough working here. The girls were a great crowd and she would genuinely miss them.

'We must all have a night out somewhere,' she said, 'and keep in touch.'

'We'll certainly do that.' Lulu smiled. 'And you must always let us know where you're performing and we'll be right there on the front row!'

Elliot hadn't been seen for several days. She knew he was in the building because news of his activities filtered down to their level. Changes were afoot in the store and he was said to be the moving force behind them. Lulu was pleased because she thought the place was being dragged into the twentieth century at last. 'They're even opening a department for new young designers at last. And about time too. Good old Elliot Priest,' she said.

'*Old?*' One of the girls raised an eyebrow.

'*Good?*' Someone else did likewise.

They all laughed, but even the most gossipy among them couldn't link Elliot with any specific name, though there were plenty of rumours going the rounds.

Rachel tried not to listen. She had made her decision and that was that. Even the blandishments of her admirers at the Manhattan couldn't deflect her from the single-minded course she was pursuing. And the blandishments were many.

Night after night there were flowers from the man who had sent that first enormous basket. Sometimes they were in the same style, with different colours predominating. Sometimes they were at the other extreme—simple nosegays or exquisite out-of-season snowdrops, or roses, blood-red, speaking of eternal love.

'I can always find out who he is,' Ray suggested as he once more handed over a cardless offering.

'Primroses!' she exclaimed. 'How can he get primroses at this time of year?' She raised enormous blue eyes. 'I really don't understand why he's doing it. Why doesn't he say who he is?'

'He will. And then what are you going to do?'

Rachel shrugged. 'It would seem churlish not to do something, I suppose. He must be a real romantic.' She sighed. 'Hopefully he'll just keep on sending them. Or stop.' She swung back with a little laugh. 'Perhaps he owns a flower shop, and these are his left-overs!'

It seemed that, the more glamorous her cabaret act became, the plainer she dressed when not performing. This morning when she went into work she was wearing a plain grey skirt, rather long, and flat ballet-style pumps, together with the white silk blouse of her lunch interview with Herman Ward. It had a frilled, pie-crust collar and this time she wore it with a simple string of seed-pearls. Since that lunch date she had taken to wearing her hair up every day. It suited her oval face. Without make-up or earrings she looked almost like a schoolgirl, and a prefect at that, she thought, as she caught sight of herself in the plate-glass window of the store.

She was frowning slightly as she made her way upstairs. So far she hadn't made any decision about Herman Ward's offer. The simple reason was, she had no one she could discuss his terms with apart from Ray, and he had hesitated to influence her one way or the other.

'The thing is—and I may as well be frank—I get a percentage if you go to him for making the introduction.' He looked away. 'There were others. But I feel he's one of the most reliable.'

She wondered if she should make an appointment with a solicitor and get a professional opinion? The small print outlining options and rights worried her. Somehow, though, with working a full week in the store she didn't seem to have time to get anything sorted out.

By mid-morning she was sitting with her feet up for ten minutes, having finished her displays in record time, when the same junior who had brought her a message from Hilda's secretary appeared in the doorway again. 'Mr Priest's livid. He wants you to go up at once, Rachel.'

'What has Mr Priest got to be livid about?' she demanded as laconically as she could. In reality her heart began to pound like a marathon runner's.

'He didn't say. He just said, "Get her up here at once. If she's condescended to come in today."'

Rachel was in two minds. Should she finish her coffee and then meekly do his bidding? Or should she simply remain here and pretend she hadn't got the message? No to that, she thought, for the junior would probably get it in the neck. Sighing, she finished her coffee break, then, conscious of the sympathetic glances following her out, she made her way to the lifts.

This time there was no hand on her elbow as she stepped out on to the seventh floor, nothing but an impersonal ocean of blue carpet and several imposing doors behind which she could hear absolutely nothing. She headed for the one where Elliot had offered lunch just after they met but there was no one inside so she went down the corridor, peering at all the plaques until she found one with his name on it.

Her heart was hammering unaccountably and she told herself not to be so silly. She was reacting like a schoolgirl up before the head. There was nothing he could do to her. He couldn't even give her the sack.

She tapped lightly on the door. From somewhere deep within the room came a voice ordering her to enter. Elliot was seated at the far end behind a vast expanse of polished oak. He had his back to the light so she could only guess at his expression. His jacket was thrown across the back of a chair beside him, and in his shirt-sleeves he still looked formidable, like a man getting down to business.

His manner, she discovered when she heard him greet her, was glacial. 'Sit down.' He indicated the chair in front of the desk.

She felt like declining the invitation, but a moment's reflection made her see how childish this would appear. She sat.

'Well?' he demanded.

'Sorry?' Play dumb, she thought, and anyway, I really don't know what this is all about.

'Why?' He leaned forward, his high cheekbones more pronounced as if anger had made the skin tighten. There was a moment's silence while his eyes glittered as impersonally as frost under an arctic sun.

'Why what?' she asked eventually. She tried to breathe, having found that she had been holding herself rigid throughout the pause, breath held in.

'Stop playing games for once. Why have I been handed *this*?' He held up a piece of paper.

'I don't know.' She bit her lip. 'I can't see it from here so I can't tell what it is.'

'Read it.' He skimmed the paper across the desk. Her chair was so low she had to get up so she could reach for it. As she stretched out her hand he clamped one hand hard down over the back of it, pinning it to the desk. For a moment the physical contact hit her like a bombshell. She felt a lick of flame envelope her body. With head averted she waited for him to release her.

With the same suddenness, he released her hand then got to his feet and walked rapidly over to the window. There he stood with his back to her, every taut muscle of his broad shoulders outlined under the straining cotton of his white shirt.

With trembling fingers, for she had never seen anyone in such an unaccountable, such a barely contained rage, she reached out and picked up the sheet of paper that seemed to be the cause of it all.

'It seems to be a list of employees who have either handed in their notice or been sacked,' she said in a subdued voice after she'd scanned it.

'And is your name among them?'

'I should think so.' Confused, she couldn't find it, and had to read the short list two or three times before she recognised her own name.

'So why the hell, Rachel?'

'I felt it was time to—well, I felt it was time to leave.' Her face felt drained of colour. It wasn't fair that he should make things that were difficult even more so. He was unfair.

'Is it because of *me*?' He swivelled in time to watch her expression change. He noted the colour flood her cheeks and, misunderstanding it, grunted, 'I thought so. Pace too hot for you. Can't trust yourself. So you run away. To hell with you, then. Go on, then. *Get out!*'

She placed the sheet of paper on the desk and stood looking down at it, unable to think straight. With an effort she turned towards the door.

He was across the room in two strides, barring her way, his voice a rough whisper, steel on silk, rasping, 'Couldn't you have told me yourself? Why let me find out like this?'

'I didn't think you'd——' No, she silently corrected, it wasn't true to say she thought he wouldn't notice. 'I don't know,' she finished miserably. 'Why should I have?'

He tilted her chin and she was conscious of his fingers trembling against her jawbone. *'Why should you?'* His eyes bored into hers as if to pierce through to whatever secrets lay hidden in her heart. 'Are you saying you could walk away without saying goodbye?'

She blinked, longing to shut out that lancing look, yet mesmerised too by the intensity of it.

He pressed his free hand down her spine, dragging her savagely against him as he did so. The shock that ran through her seemed to set her senses ablaze.

'Don't, Elliot——' she began, knowing already it was too late. But the reprieve did not come; desire for his touch, aroused, was not satisfied. He went on looking down at her, slowly allowing her release. He paced across the room then came back until he stood a yard in front of her. She thought it unlikely that the dynamic Elliot Priest was lost for words, but that seemed to be the case.

She waited, helplessly, not knowing what else to do, while destiny seemed to weigh the pros and cons in the balance. Eventually, as if something had been decided, Elliot gave her a slow, burning look and went to sit down behind his desk. He leaned back, looking anywhere but in her face. He seemed suddenly exhausted, as if the life had seeped out of him.

'I imagined that if I gave you time you'd see sense. But it seems I underestimated your puritan instincts.' He gave her a measuring glance that took in the flat shoes, the long grey skirt, the sensible white blouse and the neatly pleated hair.

'No make-up...? Well, it suits you. You've got the skin, as I'm sure men are constantly telling you. Seeing much of that gentleman friend of yours? I can't bring myself to call him *boy*friend——' He laughed derisively.

'Elliot, it isn't like that——'

'No, don't tell me. You're just good friends. He was your uncle, your elder brother. Your father even. No,' he corrected savagely, 'he didn't look like a farmer. Too knowing for that. Too dissipated. He didn't look like any sort of uncle a girl like you might have, either, so try another line.'

'He's an—an associate,' she stumbled over the word.

'A *close* associate, do you mean? How close, Rachel? *Very* close?' He laughed harshly again, answering his own question. 'Judging by the way he was slobbering over you all through lunch, very close indeed!'

'He was not—slobbering.' She drew herself up. 'He was merely being charming and courteous.'

'You like old-world charm, do you, Rachel? Come near me and I'll show you "old-world charm" you won't forget in a hurry.'

She tightened her lips but could find nothing to say.

'I said,' he repeated lethally soft-voiced, 'come here.'

'I don't see why I should.'

He uncoiled from his chair and moved towards her with all the contained savagery of a panther about to spring. 'Does he make love to you?' His voice shook. 'Do *you* make love to *him*?' He was touching her again, this time with just one finger, allowing it to snake a crazy path down the side of her cheek.

With a sharply indrawn breath he allowed it to slide down her neck and over the soft swell of her blouse. His lips tightened cruelly. 'Does this old-world lover of yours do this to you, Rachel? Does he touch you like this? Does he touch you here——' he cupped one of her breasts in his palm '—like this——?' He let his hand slide down to her waist, squeezing it, massaging in ever deeper intimacy the rounded curve of her thighs, then slithering his hand over her buttocks, pulling her slowly and rhythmically against him so that she felt the old inability to resist sweep over her again.

'Don't do that,' she croaked in a token protest, wishing he would stop, for she could not when she

felt the evidence of his own desire burning against
her like this. She stifled a groan. 'Don't, Elliot. I
don't know what you think you prove by this, but
please don't.'

'Move away, then,' he whispered maddeningly in
her ear. 'I'm not holding you, Rachel, you're doing
this of your own accord.'

It was true. His touch was featherlight, with no
force in it, yet it held her against him like a band
of tempered steel.

'You want me as much as I want you. We both
know it. I've given you time. I've been patient and
God knows I'm not a patient man. But I thought
things waited for were best. I'll give you time. I'll
take the pressure off. I thought what was happening between us was so powerful, so cataclysmic,
that we both needed time to get used to it, time to
find our balance—what I never expected was for
you to walk out on it. I don't see how you can!
What demon of self-punishment is leading you to
walk out, Rachel? What sort of self-inflicted joy-
lessness drives you to say no to what you really
want?'

She was swooning now. His arms, loosely holding
her, supported her weight. She felt her eyes close,
tears of longing, of love—she recognised it now—
building up behind them. But then the future swung
into focus. It taunted her. His words were honeyed
traps, designed to lead her along the primrose path.
All her dreams would be destroyed. And when he
had used her and drained her, no matter what she
had sacrificed for him, he would discard her, because for a man like him the world was full of pretty
women waiting for love.

Opening her eyes, she said, 'You only want me because you're attracted to what you can't have, Elliot. You shan't have it. You *can't*.'

His reply was to sink his lips against hers, to savage her soft mouth in a brief plundering, eyes closed, veiling his bitter anger. With tension marking his features he began to let her go, moving away little by little until he reached the limit of his ability to leave her entirely. She could feel the heat of desire from him drawing her back towards him. If he had reached out again she would have been powerless to stop the words of love tumbling from her lips, but reprieve lay in his own pride and anger and some other emotion blinding him to his own power. It made him draw back still further until at last the contact was broken.

He stood behind the desk once more, picked up his discarded jacket, fumbled in the pockets, put it on, and stood again, undecided, gazing without a word until at last he broke the silence with a harsh exclamation, saying, 'I've probably broken every rule in the book for employer-employee relations. Are you going to take me to court for sexual harassment? I wouldn't blame you.' He looked as disgusted with himself as he was with her.

'I simply want to walk out of here and forget this ever happened. Forget we ever met.' Her voice dropped to a whisper.

He waved a hand towards the door. Reading it, she turned blindly and walked out. He said nothing more, and she closed the door between them with a sense of deep despair.

CHAPTER SIX

COMPARED to the grey gloom hanging over Rachel's daytime world, Zia's existence was nothing if not multi-coloured. Rising from the ashes of Rachel's life, Zia was a phoenix, a creature of flame and brilliance, an incandescence that spread its glow everywhere. She would arrive early at the club these days, as if something drove her to cut short the painful hours of Rachel's existence and embrace instead the gaudy dream that awaited her as Zia.

In the privacy of her dressing-room that evening she stripped to the skin, catching sight of the pale, vulnerable form in the mirror. Then she reached for the exotic concoction of hot pinks and cherry-reds she was to wear that night. An image had evolved without her even trying and now when she donned her stage clothes she looked as sultry and sinful and as far removed from Rachel as it was possible to get.

The silk slithered over her head, concealing and revealing her pearly skin in unexpected places as the diaphanous material swirled with every gesture. The neckline plunged low, the bodice was delicately boned, lifting and shaping her firm breasts beneath the thin fabric.

She slid into a pair of gold sandals with impossibly high heels that made walking a problem. But then, she smiled grimly, she wasn't going far, was she? Ten paces from the wings to the centre of the stage. A little provocative step or two when the music commanded. A teetering step to the edge of the spotlight to accept the acclaim at the end. Then back into the darkness.

She lifted the tight skirt to thigh-level so she could sit at the dressing-table and began to work on her make-up. It was taking her nearly an hour or more these days. As she worked, skimming on layer after layer of silk foundation, highlighter, shader, blusher, powder as fine as spun silk on her already perfect features, she talked herself into her role. Then she shaped and deepened her eyes with a skill taught to her by a friend in the make-up department. She added two layers of false eyelashes, outlined her lips in scarlet, glossed and buffed and perfected until the transformation was almost complete.

By now she was coming round to the idea of having her hair lightened, growing it, having a perm perhaps to give it body, but in the meantime she allowed the hairpieces to become her trade-mark. Tonight it was a wild confection of real and false hair, plaited and curled, an outrageous sexy provocative coif that emphasised the gamine in her but hinted at an all-female sensuality too.

It was play-acting. She thought that was obvious to everyone. But one or two, like Henry, like the mystery man who had sent the flowers, seemed to take it seriously. Tonight was the first night she didn't care. Rachel might lurk when the night was over, ready to reclaim her for the land of the half-dead in which she existed by day, but the night— tonight—belonged to Zia.

Her cue came over the intercom and she made her way through the shadowed passage towards the bright oval of the tiny stage.

Her theme tune had already started and she hesitated in the wings for a moment, frightened to go on, yet more frightened to stay in the shadows where no one knew her name, where love was only another name for heartbreak. Out there, in the bright circle of the stage, her name was known and loved and heartbreak was only the theme of a song. Now, as her melody lilted around her, she still hesitated.

From her vantage-point she could see the boys in the band. Dapper as always in dinner-jackets, with brilliantined hair and rings on their fingers, they were her team. Her knights in chivalry. Once when a drunk had tried to get on stage to kiss her the drummer had materialised from nowhere, leading the man off to face a polite ejection from the premises.

Tonight, she thought, conscious of the unseen audience packed tight in the darkness beyond the footlights, she desperately needed their protective, collective presence. She needed all their help to get her through the night.

It was late when the last note died away on a whisper of sound. There was a brief pause, then the applause began, building to a tidal wave of emotion swamping them all. Zia had tears streaming down her cheeks. She turned, blinded by them, blinded by the emotion the words of the song had aroused.

He was so right. He had accused her of being driven by some self-torturing demon. And she was. Anyone else would have forced themselves to forget the love they had deliberately rejected. But she couldn't forget. Every note of every song was for the tragedy of lost love, for lovers the world over parted by the hand of fate, for her own love lost . . . for Elliot.

A vision of the desert that lay in wait, the lifetime without him, the endless years ahead, reared up to taunt her. When she came off stage she hurried straight to her dressing-room, closing the door, cutting off the applause as it echoed hollowly on and on without end. Tonight wasn't the night for encores. She collapsed on a chair in front of the mirror, her eyes reflecting back all the emptiness she felt inside.

Was it worth it? she asked herself. Was anything worth this hell? Would success assuage the torment of loving and losing? She doubted it.

When Henry sent his usual love token to her dressing-room, this time she put out a trembling hand.

'May as well open it,' she suggested to the waiter as he was about to leave with the unopened champagne. He did a double-take.

'Yes, I mean it!' She gave Zia's throaty laugh, reluctant to leave the safety of her disguise. She picked up the red rose and placed it in the cleft of her bosom. 'What's he like, this Henry? As nice-looking as Ray says?'

'I don't know your taste, Zia.' The young waiter smiled. 'He's certainly not an ogre.'

'Tell him I'll join him for ten minutes.' She turned back to the mirror to freshen her make-up, cutting off the waiter's exclamation of surprise.

He left at once and in a moment or two returned with the terse reply, 'He can't believe his luck. You'd better get out there quickly, otherwise he's likely to have a heart attack with the suspense,' And as she left he added, 'You've made his day.'

'Let's hope he can make mine!' She lifted one shoulder. Rachel would have blushed and wondered what the fuss was about. Zia gave a world-weary yawn. Now for it, she whispered aloud, bracing herself before she stepped out, almost as if she were going back on stage. Ray's fatherly hand in the small of her back propelled her forward to make the introduction, and stayed too, keeping a protective eye on things.

Henry was fortyish with the slightly overweight good looks of a man who lives well with no responsibilities other than to himself. He had a pleasant, unassuming smile and she couldn't help being charmed. He was so sweet, so attentive and so obviously adored Zia. She had warned Ray to give her an opening to make her departure after ten minutes or so and on cue he rose to his feet, one hand on the back of her chair.

'I hope you won't neglect our other guests,' he murmured, spreading an apologetic hand. Henry rose to his feet with alacrity, holding her chair, helping Ray shepherd her towards another table as if she were made of fine porcelain. When it became obvious he wasn't included in this new round of introductions he went back to his own party, smiling, besotted, obviously grateful for any crumbs Zia would throw his way.

The quiet voice in her ear was Ray saying, 'This, I suspect, is the man who sends the flowers.' It brought her head lifting, a smile already in place. Then she felt her blood turn to ice. Strength fled from out of her and she stumbled, beginning to sink like a rag doll until Ray's arm came discreetly round her waist to support her.

A spindly gold chair appeared and she sank down on to it, her head averted from the man who had risen at her arrival with one hand outstretched in greeting.

No, not Elliot! No, no! she repeated to herself. Not him. Please... not Elliot! But it was.

Slowly she raised her head as control reasserted itself. In the candlelight he looked very different from the last time they had confronted each other. His expression now was by contrast almost gentle, and in his dinner-jacket, with his black tie slightly awry, he seemed more endearing than ever. Only the brilliant clarity of his eyes hinted at how formidable he could be as an adversary. She waited for him to exclaim in derision at her presence, her own final bitter words coming back now to taunt her, but he was smiling blandly, with apparently nothing but delighted surprise on his features as if everything was well between them.

'Zia, you do me an honour,' he was already taking one of her hands in his, 'I'd given up hope of ever meeting you.' He bowed over her hand. 'I suppose I should have put a name to the flowery tributes,' he dismissed them as nothings, 'but I never intended they should lead to a meeting. It was,' he went on with negligent courtesy, 'beyond my wildest hope.'

So that was the game, she thought. What an actor! 'I rarely meet my fans,' she said coolly, matching him tone for tone. 'Usually I feel so exhausted after a performance I need only to rest.'

'You put so much into it,' he agreed, 'so much emotion. You obviously live life in top gear to shame the rest of us who can only manage to chug along in first.'

'I'm sure that's untrue of you,' she murmured, unsure where the conversation was leading. Why didn't he address her as Rachel? Ask her what the hell she was doing, parading around in a wig and fancy-dress?

But he went on in the same vein. 'Zia,' he said, 'I have to confess, I first caught your performance quite by chance. I came here on a whim, a wild-goose chase as it turned out, due to what one might call a *folie d'amour*——' He paused, frowned, smiled suddenly, the soldier-blue eyes sharpening. 'The words of the song struck me as strikingly apt at the time...'

'Folie d'amour?' Her lips tightened.

'Something drew me to return and it was then, I suppose, that you caught me in your spell.' He chuckled in that familiar, teasing way Rachel had grown to love. Only now it made her want to hit him. How dared he dismiss Rachel as a *folie d'amour*? But then, that was what she'd known he would do all along, especially when he tired of her and decided it was time for pastures new.

Yet she couldn't get to grips with what was happening now. Did he intend to go on all evening pretending she was Zia?

Ray saved the situation. 'I really think we must move on, Zia. I believe you have a taxi waiting?'

'I was rather hoping you would join me for a late meal,' Elliot broke in. 'I understand you performers prefer to eat after a show rather than before?'

'I—oh, no, I couldn't——' She bit her lip and pretended to inspect her fingernails. Her legs wouldn't obey the simple command to carry her away out of his range. Her eyes when she turned them on Ray implored his help.

He crooked an arm under hers. 'Time to go.' He brought her to her feet.

'Thank you for the flowers,' she said to Elliot over her shoulder. Somehow she managed to walk with a reasonable show of assurance to the seclusion of the corridor backstage then she stopped, leaning weakly against Ray with no fight left.

'You all right, sweetheart?' He frowned.

She nodded, avoiding his glance.

'You put a hell of a lot into your performance tonight. I'll get you a nice drink of milk and put you in that taxi.'

'Oh, Ray, if you only knew...' No one would know how much she had put into her performance. And that included the last ten minutes. Why was Elliot playing with her? Why hadn't he told her he knew she was Zia? Why hadn't he mentioned the flowers when he saw her at the store? Even a casual remark like, 'Did they arrive safely?'—anything but this pretence. As if he didn't know who she really was!

There were only ten days left of her notice and she felt a mixture of relief and sorrow. It was tiring doing both jobs, but on the other hand the business of the store kept her from brooding over Elliot. He was around, a fact which made the days seem as fraught as a passage across a minefield even though they didn't meet face to face. She had expected, indeed, longed for, some come-back from their meeting at the Manhattan—a second chance of some sort—but nothing happened. The following night his 'flowery tribute', as he jokingly called it, turned up as usual. It was a sheaf of roses so dark, they were almost black. And so it continued, but with never a card, as if he was reluctant to commit himself in writing.

Inevitably they had to come face to face in the store. Rachel had just finished dressing one of the windows and was feeling hot and dishevelled. She was wearing black matador trousers and a loose striped man's shirt and her hair, longer now and gently streaked, was pulled back in a black ribbon. As usual she wore no make-up. Elliot was crossing one of the sales floors in the company of a tall, extremely self-confident and glamorous woman a little older than himself. They were deep in conversation. Rachel, her arms full of the paraphernalia from the window, had to step to one side to avoid being trampled. She was scowling over the top of some boxes teetering in her arms when Elliot noticed her. He said something to his companion and they both came to a leisurely halt.

'Having problems, Rachel?' His voice held a deliberate edge. Employer to slightly useless employee, she registered.

Nettled, she gave him a haughty stare then couldn't stop her glance flicking towards his companion. 'I can manage, thank you, sir,' she said with just the slightest ironic emphasis on the word 'sir'.

Its delicacy was not lost on Elliot. 'Surely you can find someone to——' he paused in a most suggestive way before adding innocently '—give you a helping hand....?' He paused again. Smiled. 'I don't like to see you getting all hot and bothered.'

'I'm all right,' she muttered, knowing he detected the blush that was already beginning at the image his words forced to mind.

He gave a glance towards the cool figure standing beside him. 'I'm just going up to the hospitality room on seventh, otherwise I'd get some help for you.'

'I can manage quite well. I always do,' she replied. 'Thank you for your concern, *sir*.'

'It's my duty,' he remarked laconically with a hand under the elbow of his companion as he strolled away.

Rachel continued towards the escalator, wondering why her heart was thudding so much, and if she was crazy to imagine anything going on beneath the ordinariness of their exchange. She couldn't work him out. He had obviously discarded all thoughts of pursuing Rachel, for which fact she ought to feel grateful, but the flowers still kept coming for Zia. If he wanted to confuse her he was succeeding admirably.

That night she sat with Henry for a few moments after she finished. She had decided to go ahead and sign the contract with Southern Artists and Herman Ward was in the audience. She felt Henry afforded

some protection, as Herman was hardly likely to
start making suggestive remarks about dinner *à
deux* with a third party in earshot. Ray couldn't be
expected to accompany her all the time. He had
other guests to talk to. Henry, she realised, had been
pursuing her for so long that he hadn't yet registered that she might be available for something more
than distant adoration. Not that she was. But, given
her proximity at the little gilt table at which they
were now sitting, he might have been forgiven for
thinking so.

They chatted about this and that. Zia bubbled
in a way Rachel could not have. It was all lightness
and banter. Beneath it she was aware of Elliot, a
rather bored look on his face, leaning back on his
gilt chair, a long glass held casually in one hand as
he watched the trio going through their paces. He
was accompanied, she noticed, by the same woman
she had seen in the store that afternoon.

No accounting for taste, she thought unjustly,
remembering his own reaction to Herman Ward.

Soon she got up to make her way backstage to
change ready for home. She had gone only two
paces along the corridor when she heard her name.
Her night-name.

'Zia?'

Turning she saw Elliot sauntering casually down
the corridor towards her. 'You left so suddenly, I
didn't get chance to invite you over. I thought you
might have joined me anyway?' he said.

'You're with someone,' she remarked in tight,
Rachel tones.

'Only wining and dining a business colleague,'
he told her. He looked impossibly sophisticated in

his ecru dinner-jacket, just a little wildness in his dark hair lending him that lethally untamed look she had so far been unable to forget. Instinctively she flattened herself against the wall as he approached. Rachel crowding uppermost in her mind and warning her to run. But Zia stepped smoothly to the fore.

'Two's company,' she whispered with a provocative flutter of her eyelashes. Now is the moment he can bring the two halves of my life together at last, she thought wildly as he bent over her.

'Three can be company sometimes,' he murmured. 'Won't you come and join us?'

'I really am exhausted, you know. I need to get home to bed,' she stalled in confusion.

'Bed?' His eyes smouldered. 'With a husband in it?'

Rachel felt floored. He knew she wasn't married. 'What makes you say a thing like that?' she asked huskily.

'Isn't it true?'

She looked blank until he went on, 'Surely a woman like you has a man waiting for her...?'

'I——' She licked her lips, unsure how to proceed. 'I like to keep my life simple,' she managed, not realising how provocative she looked as, suddenly shy, she twirled her fingers in the turbulent tresses of her hairpiece.

He placed one hand on the wall behind her head. It made her think of the time in the lift when he had done just that as a prelude to the kiss she still dreamed about. The slight opening of her lips, her eyes widening in remembered anticipation, made him go still. 'Life sounds rather lonely for you,' he murmured thickly, eyes never wavering from her mouth.

'I—no, I——' She licked her lips, unconsciously making them look even softer and more desirable than ever.

With a small smile like a contestant in a game of skill, Elliot lowered his own lips to within an inch of Zia's and paused, savouring the inevitable *coup de grâce*.

Rachel was transfixed. What would Zia do? Rachel would submit. She would let him lead her wherever he chose. The fight had left her. She wanted him. She loved him. But Zia? Ambitious Zia?

He murmured her name.

It gave her something to cling on to. She licked her lips again out of sheer nervousness, imagining the sweet warmth of his mouth on hers, then, after a prolonged moment of indecision, she averted her head.

'I really don't think——'

'That this is an appropriate time? No, neither do I. Forgive me.' He slipped a hand into his top pocket and drew out a card. 'Contact me some time. We'll have dinner somewhere special.' He stepped back, a cool smile playing round his lips. 'There is something—I have the most peculiar feeling about you...' He frowned, then gave her a brisk smile. 'No matter. I expect to hear from you—make it soon!'

Then he left.

Rachel stood for long minutes staring after him. There was only one thing she could think. *He didn't know.* He really didn't know who she was. Everything he said confirmed his ignorance about her true identity!

She returned to her dressing-room and peered at herself in the full-length mirror. She switched off the dazzle of bulbs around the dressing-mirror and then she understood. In the false hair, the outrageous stage garb, she looked like nothing Rachel could even dream of. Even the high heels changed her, making her seem slimmer than she really was, and the dress accentuated curves that Rachel's plain workaday garb only concealed. As for her face, the false eyelashes were a transformation, darkening her cornflower blue eyes, lending them an air of mystery that hinted she was a woman with a past... It was the most effective disguise she could have devised.

What now? she thought. Shall I go on playing at being Zia? Could she get back what she had thoughtlessly thrown away in the guise of another woman? Elliot no longer cared for Rachel. But if he could care for Zia, wouldn't that be just as good?

She bumped into him in the store first thing next morning. She felt pale and tired and must have looked washed out, for he gave her a sardonic glance from across the corridor and bore down on her at once, his whole manner changed from the previous night. 'Lover-boy keeping you up late at night, is he?' He spoke aggressively, eyes bleak with dislike. 'You've got rings under your eyes, Rachel. Didn't Mummy tell you to get enough beauty sleep?'

'I get enough sleep, thank you.'

'I don't.'

'That's your affair.'

'I have sleepless nights. I wonder why.'

'Too much nightclubbing,' she retorted.

'Yes. But I haven't seen you at the Manhattan recently. Found newer, more genteel pastures?'

'I'm not interested in—going out.'

'To be honest, neither am I. Waste of time, isn't it?'

'Why do it, then?'

'Perhaps I hope to see you there one of these nights—so we can get on the floor and pretend to dance as we did once before. Perhaps you've forgotten that——' He gazed into her eyes. 'I wish I could. I wish I weren't still tormented by the memory of your body pressing against mine as if you wanted——' He broke off abruptly. 'So there it is, you must be pleased with yourself.'

If she hadn't known how he had almost taken Zia's lips she would have been convinced he really was as lovelorn as he pretended, but last night was branded on her memory. 'I'm sure you've found other consolations at the Manhattan,' she couldn't help jibing.

'Sure.' He gave a lazy laugh. 'With the fabulous Zia, you mean?'

'Have you won your bet?' she asked, pushed by some demon to see how he would respond.

He shrugged, a fleeting smile playing round his lips. 'I'd forgotten that. But yes, she seems to be a very warm and generous woman. Almost irresistible.' He paused. 'There's something about her that strikes a chord...' Then he gave another harder laugh. 'But don't worry, Rachel, she's even less my type than I am yours. I prefer my women unspoiled. Since meeting you I guess I'm doomed to go for the innocent milkmaid type.'

'So you can spoil their innocence?' she burst out. 'Or because you imagine that type is too naïve to see through you? On that count, if what you say is right, Zia should be your match!'

'A cabaret artiste?' He raised an eyebrow. 'I don't think so. While she may be fun for a while, I couldn't see it lasting. To quote you, we're worlds apart.' He chuckled. 'Can you imagine her at the opera?'

'I can't imagine *you* at the opera.' Her voice was full of venom, the desire to hurt him as he had just hurt her, albeit unwittingly, being uppermost. But as a taunt it fell flat.

'You don't know me, then.'

'You don't know me either,' she muttered.

'I know you're afraid of letting go for some reason. You like to play at being Rachel the prude. Who is it supposed to impress? It doesn't impress *me*!' He swivelled suddenly as if tired of this meaningless conversation and started to walk away.

His words had aroused such an opposition in her heart that she heard herself call after him, 'If you stopped thinking of women as types for you to pick and choose among, maybe you'd have more——'

'Yes?' He spun to face her. 'Maybe I'd what? Have more *success*?' he taunted. 'I can assure you, Rachel, I have all the success I can handle. It's only with you I'm willing to bow out gracefully and admit defeat. Fortunately, there are plenty more fish in the sea.'

As if to confirm what he meant, two secretaries went past, self-consciously undulating when they noticed him. He allowed his glance to trail them down the corridor before turning back to Rachel with a thin smile. 'You see? You're only harming yourself by saying no to life. Poor frightened Rachel. You don't know what you're missing!' He swivelled and made his way after the two secretaries, leaving Rachel to fume and snarl helplessly to herself.

She felt like blurting everything out to Lulu when she got back upstairs but was afraid she would say she was crazy to have turned him down in the first place.

She knew it wasn't true that she was frightened of life, and nor was it in her nature to say no all the time. It was simply that she knew she would never be happy to be an also-ran. She had to give her singing career all she'd got. What she hadn't realised was how great the self-sacrifice was going to be.

She wanted to give her heart to Elliot, but how could she, when she knew an affair with him would turn her life upside-down? For her it would have to be a serious commitment, something neither of them in their different ways wanted.

And now, wasn't she trapped in that decision—knowing what he thought about her other self? He had rejected the goody-goody Rachel, and he had revealed his short-term interest in Zia too.

CHAPTER SEVEN

RACHEL was in the stock-room when she heard the door open, and a familiar voice said, 'I saw lover-boy at the Manhattan last night. I think he's two-timing you, Rachel.' The soft tones caressed her while dropping poison in her ear.

She couldn't help but smile when she turned. 'Why do you think *I* care, Elliot? It was probably his wife. And why not? I told you, he's nothing to me. If you're trying to hurt me I'm afraid you've failed.'

'Hurt?' For a moment he looked stunned. 'That was the last thing on my mind. I thought I was *saving* you from hurt. It's a relief to know you're not involved with him after all . . . I couldn't help thinking there must be somebody in the background with a hold over you. I'm glad it's not him.'

Her eyes softened. A heartbeat went by during which there seemed to be no barriers between them. Then inevitably he remembered her rejection and she saw them come back up again.

'Excuse me, for a moment I forgot you didn't believe in *relationships*,' he said in stilted tones. 'It's an impossible thought to get one's head around.' He flipped the pen he'd been using into his top pocket and snapped shut the file he was resting on the stock-room counter.

'Where's Lulu?' he asked. 'I want to go over these with her.' He tapped a sheaf of notes. He seemed to be poking his nose into every aspect of the store and Rachel couldn't quench her admiration for his ability to get things done. She wondered what he would move on to once he'd got the store organised the way he wanted it. One thing was for sure, she wouldn't be here to find out. Her last day was looming ever closer.

She went to find Lulu for him.

Ray was looking rather downcast when she went in that night. He was slumped behind his desk as she popped her head round the door to say hello in as cheery a voice as she could muster before she went to change. But when she saw his face she stopped.

'Ray, what is it?' she asked in consternation.

'Oh, it's nothing, love.'

She noticed the whisky glass on the desk beside him. It was unlike him to take a drink except out of politeness to his guests. Even then he was known to nurse the same small Scotch all night. She came right inside. 'Can I get you anything? An aspirin or something?' she asked.

He looked up with a bemused smile. 'Aspirin won't help. It's my wife, love. She had a heart attack this afternoon. Not a big one, but enough to scare the pants off me.' He sighed. 'I was just thinking I ought to take her away somewhere relaxing. She's had enough of London.' He looked up. 'Don't worry. I'm still in shock. The doctors assure me she's going to be all right.'

Rachel went into her dressing-room when she realised there was nothing she could do and later on she saw Ray apparently back on form entertaining some customers in his usual urbane manner.

Her performance and the applause that followed seemed almost routine now. So too did the twenty minutes or so she spent afterwards with Henry. He seemed quite content to let the relationship remain as it was, perhaps deflected from further ambition by Zia's manner, perhaps because it was enough to be seen with her, the envy of every man in the club, so Ray said.

Elliot was there again, as if he couldn't keep away. She noticed him as soon as he arrived and when she found herself lingering at Henry's table she wondered if it was because of the perverse pain it brought her, to find herself so close to, though in reality so far from, Elliot's side. His presence was like something touching her all over, and she wondered why nobody else seemed to be aware of it. He was with the same woman she had seen before, the so-called business colleague. They were chatting casually, and even jealousy couldn't make Rachel see them as anything but the old friends he'd said they were.

He hadn't approached her in her guise as Zia since handing her his card and she wondered what would happen if she took him up on his offer... apart from having her true identity revealed, of course. When he caught her watching him he raised his glass in a toast, but made no further attempt to seek her out.

Thursdays were usually the day she redid the windows ready for the weekend, and Rachel came prepared to get on as usual even though it was her last day. But Lulu had already arrived and there was a new girl with her.

'Meet your successor. Sharon, this is Rachel, whose place you'll be taking.' After they had chatted for a few minutes and Lulu had given Sharon a window to dress she said, 'Come on, Rachel. I'm sure Sharon doesn't want us breathing down her neck on her first morning. Let's go and have a coffee in the crush bar and tie up a few loose ends.'

Feeling slightly guilty at having a break before she had had chance to do any work, Rachel followed Lulu up to the third floor.

The loose ends, so called, were disposed of in a few minutes, then Rachel realised Lulu had something else on her mind. 'So how are things in the rest of your life?' she began, fingering the rim of her coffee-cup. 'You're putting on a brave enough face but I feel I know you well enough by now to guess something's wrong.'

'What on earth could be wrong?' flared Rachel, then, as she saw Lulu's sympathetic expression, her anger subsided at once. 'I'm sorry,' she muttered. 'You're quite right, you know you are. I should have realised I couldn't get anything past you!'

'It's him, isn't it? Elliot?' Lulu frowned. 'I know everybody gossips about him, but he's not the rake he's made out to be. He's just a friendly guy doing his job, that's all, and sometimes people take him more seriously than he intends.'

'Do they?'

'Not you. I don't mean you. You're the one he seeks out, Rachel. I think he's genuinely interested in you. But you seem to distrust him. I can't understand why.'

'Maybe there's nothing to understand——'

'And it's none of my business anyway. I'm sorry, love.' She looked thoughtful. 'It's just that it helps to talk to somebody sometimes, and I know you haven't been in town long enough to build up a circle of friends you can unburden yourself to.'

'It's not my style to unburden myself,' Rachel replied abruptly. Tears were beginning to crowd behind her eyes, but she fought them back. 'It's really quite simple, Lulu. I want to be a top singer. I'm going to be. *Nobody's* going to get in my way. It doesn't leave time for heavy relationships. And if you tell me people need people, like Ros, I shall scream.'

'And what else?' asked Lulu, staring her full in the face.

'What do you mean, what else?'

'Your mind tells you one thing, but where Elliot's concerned, your heart tells you another... is that it?'

'I wish you'd go away and leave me in peace,' muttered Rachel, turning away. As Lulu bit her lip Rachel regretted having to rebuff her. 'He doesn't want Rachel because she's a prude and not into casual affairs,' she blurted out, 'but what he doesn't yet know is that I'm also Zia.' Then she told her how he had apparently failed to guess the secret of her double identity—and what he had then said about Zia.

'But how can you be sure he doesn't know who you are?' asked Lulu, when Rachel finished.

'Because surely he would have said something by now?'

'I think he said enough if he said what you said he said about Zia!' remarked Lulu, somewhat tortuously.

'Obviously he meant it, because he hasn't tried to chat her—I mean me—up since then,' said Rachel. She had been unable to bring herself to mention the actual kiss—any of the kisses—but it hadn't altered the gist of what she'd confessed.

'My advice, for what it's worth,' said Lulu slowly after a pause, 'is to take him up on the offer of a date. Go to the opera with him or something, for heaven's sake.' She leaned forward, her eyes gleaming. 'Go as Zia. Prove to him she isn't the shallow creature he seems to imagine. Then admit your true identity. You can have it both ways—the taste and discrimination of Rachel, the voluptuousness of Zia...' She sat back in triumph.

Rachel shook her head. 'You don't understand. You're treating it all as a game.'

'I'm not.' Lulu puckered her brow. 'But I do know you couldn't sing the blues the way you do if your heart weren't breaking. And I'm suggesting a way out.'

Still Rachel shook her head. She felt there was only one sure, safe thing to hold on to in the storm that had swept into her life ever since Elliot had come into it. 'I'm a singer,' she whispered. 'I have to hang on to that thought because after Elliot finishes with me I would have less than nothing.'

'Why should he finish with you?'

'We've been over this,' she replied wearily. 'Because he doesn't take love seriously. Look at the way he's sending Zia all those flowers.'

Lulu drew a circle in spilled sugar grains on the formica table-top. 'I have a theory about that. I think it's subliminal.'

Rachel frowned.

'I mean, I think he has a subliminal recognition that you're really Rachel. It's just that it hasn't yet emerged into his conscious mind.'

Rachel almost smiled. 'I must say, Lulu, you don't give up easily.'

'And you're probably one of the most stubborn creatures I've ever met. The guy's obviously mad for you.' She got up. 'Still, if you don't want him that's your decision.' She glanced over Rachel's shoulder. 'You can explain it all in person, anyway, 'cos here he comes!' With a little smile she picked up her bag and left.

CHAPTER EIGHT

STARTLED, Rachel looked over her shoulder. Sure enough, Elliot himself was sauntering from behind the service counter towards them. He came directly over and Lulu gave him a brief greeting as she went out.

Rachel tried to avoid his glance but he sat down in the newly vacated chair opposite. 'So,' he began, 'have you rethought your decision to leave?'

When she shook her head, he went on, 'Got anything exciting lined up?' He eyed her beetroot face with interest.

She tried to avert her head and mumbled something like, 'Maybe.'

'You mean you're still doing the rounds of interviews?' He narrowed his glance. 'You're not running away from here merely to become unemployed, are you, Rachel?'

She shook her head, relieved to feel the hot blush begin to recede from her cheeks. 'I shall be all right,' she replied shortly. She made as if to get up but Elliot put out a restraining hand.

'Stay. There's no need to go dashing off.'

'I really ought to get back and see how Lulu's coping with the new girl,' she said.

'Very well, I imagine, knowing Lulu. Soon it'll no longer be your concern, will it?'

'I suppose not——'

'In fact, nothing to do with this store is going to be your concern, is it?'

'No—I——'

'Nothing?'

She blinked.

'I said, nothing, Rachel?'

'I——' She bit her lip. 'I don't know what you're getting at.'

'You know damn well I shall miss seeing you around,' he growled. 'At least during working hours I've always known where I could locate you—I nearly said "lay my hands on you" but that wouldn't be quite correct, would it?'

Remembering the way he had 'laid his hands' on her previously, she blushed again.

'You look so sweet. Blushing. Innocent... Too good to be true,' he added thoughtfully. 'I'm not going to let you just walk away...' He reached out and clasped his hand over hers where it lay on the table. 'It's fortunate I caught sight of you in here. I was just on my way down to find you. I have some business to attend to and I'd like you to come with me.'

'Business?'

'That makes it all right, doesn't it? One of the directors asking you for assistance?'

'But——'

'You can hardly refuse. I am your employer and I'm paying for your time until six o'clock this evening.'

'Eight,' she said. 'It's late-night closing again.'

He banged the side of his hand. 'Better still. Come on. Get your coat. Let's go.'

'My coat?' She was already standing up.

'It may be chilly. Be quick. I'll be waiting at the staff entrance.'

Wondering if they were going far, Rachel did as he asked, popping her head in to tell Lulu what she was doing on her way out. Her feelings were in tumult again—wanting to be with Elliot and yet frightened of what it might lead to as well. When she reached the glass entrance doors she could see him already waiting on the other side. For a moment her heart lurched with love. He looked so cool, so tough and decisive, yet there was a vulnerable air about him too, something that made her want to reach out and hold him in her arms. She was beginning to suspect she had hurt his feelings, that underneath the humorous exterior was a vulnerable man. Or maybe it was just his pride that was hurt, she wondered uncertainly. He turned then and caught sight of her.

A smile spread evenly over his features at once, making his eyes dance. 'Good girl,' he said, 'that was quick.' He tucked her hand into his and led her round the corner into a side-street. The company limousine was waiting, its engine running already. Feeling rather underdressed for such a grand vehicle, Rachel stepped inside.

'I don't suppose you carry your passport with you?' Elliot asked mysteriously, confounding her.

'Well—no——'

'Right, then—direct the driver to your place first,' he commanded. 'I presume it's up to date.'

'Yes, but——'

'Come on, we haven't got all day!' He smiled at her and, feeling bemused, she recited her address. Having run inside and collected the apparently necessary document, she got back in the car and at once the driver set off, conveying them speedily through the West End and towards the Docks. Soon he was driving the car up to the entrance to the City airport.

'But where are we going, Elliot?' Rachel's face was flushed with something other than embarrassment now.

Elliot gave her an enigmatic smile. 'You'll see.'

'But I thought we were simply going to offices in town!' she exclaimed.

'Nothing so dull. It is your last day, after all...' He paused and added thickly, 'It's *our* last day. OK? Think of it as a day out of time.'

She felt a lump in her throat at the thought that she would never see him again, and couldn't answer.

Mistaking her silence for opposition, he said, 'Don't begrudge me one day, Rachel. I shan't ask anything else of you.'

She gulped and turned away. Her voice was small when she replied, 'Of course I shan't begrudge it. You've got it all wrong.'

He pressed two fingers against her lips. 'Let's make a pact here and now—no soul-searching, nothing heavy, let's simply enjoy what life has to offer and forget tomorrow. Is that agreed?'

She nodded as he let his fingers fall from her lips. That was so like him. To break her heart and not even know it. Live for today. She gave a strangled little laugh. 'For today, then, a day out of time.'

Biting back her feelings, she gave him a brilliant smile as he tucked her hand in his. Zia had taught her how to act—now she would put up her best performance ever. He led her through the departure lounge to a small aircraft on the tarmac. It bore the company logo and she had no need to act as a small gasp of surprise escaped her.

'Up into the wide blue yonder!' He was plainly delighted with her reaction to the private plane and, when they were securely seated, he turned to her, his own face suffused with a glow she had rarely seen.

'I have a very short meeting to attend——' he indicated the briefcase lying in the rack in front of him '——but after that our time's our own.'

'But I have to be back tonight,' she warned, her mind suddenly filled with the ramifications of simply flying off heaven knew where with him...

'I'll qualify that last statement,' he said, allaying her fears at once. 'Our time's our own until eight o'clock. That's when your employment with me comes to an end. Will that suit you?' His eyes were like two chips of blue ice when he saw the doubt in her eyes.

Feeling obscurely guilty, she nodded. 'I'll have to trust you, won't I?' she mumbled, trying to avoid his glance.

'I assure you I can be trusted, contrary to what you seem to imagine, Rachel.' His voice was as cold as his glance. She was sorry she had destroyed that dancing warmth that had appeared only a few seconds ago and slipped her hand in his, unable to tell him that it was herself she couldn't trust, not with the raging desire for him coursing so shamelessly through every fibre of her being.

He carefully removed her hand. 'I'm afraid I'm going to have to read through some notes. You can occupy yourself until we land?'

She bit her lip and turned to look out of the window. She saw the dirty grey of southern England with its pall of cloud give way to the khaki of the open sea. True to his word, Elliot opened some files and at once became immersed.

Rachel tried to tell which way they were flying but now they were crossing a blank stretch of muddy-looking water. Was it the Channel or was it the North Sea? Soon shipping became more numerous and later low-lying sand-banks appeared on the horizon, looking like whales in all that expanse of grey. Eventually they were flying low over a flat coastline and not until she saw the first windmills did she guess where they were.

Elliot was still engrossed in his notes and as the plane started to lose height he snapped his files shut and looked at his watch. 'Schiphol,' he told her. 'We've made excellent time.'

She blinked in the bright sunlight when they eventually climbed out of the plane. A car was waiting and they were soon being driven through the suburbs of Amsterdam. 'It *is* Amsterdam, isn't it?' She turned to him, scarcely able to believe this was happening.

'Been here before?'

'Never!' She opened her eyes wide. 'It's like a picture-book. I still can't believe it's real! It's beautiful!'

'So are you.' He turned abruptly as if he wished he hadn't spoken.

When they alighted at a hotel in the city centre he held a door for her, saying, 'I shall be an hour at the very outside. You can wait in the coffee-shop for me if you like.'

'I'd like to explore a little,' she told him eagerly.

'Will you be safe by yourself?'

'Why ever not?'

He pulled her briefly against him and kissed her forehead. 'Make a note of the hotel, then, in case you have to ask directions. Most people speak English so you shouldn't have any problems. And, Rachel——' He paused and she wondered what he was going to say, but all he said was, 'Try not to be late back. We haven't much time left and I don't want to waste a minute of it. Let's agree on twelve prompt, right?'

She glanced at her watch. 'Twelve,' she agreed.

He strode off across the marble hall in what was a rather grand hotel on traditional lines. He looked wonderful, she thought, still glowing after that brief kiss. Then she shuddered. It was a bitter-sweet feeling, knowing their hours together were numbered. But it was better than nothing, and today she would follow Elliot's own advice. She would live as if there were no tomorrow.

First she wandered down the main street, looking in the big stores, but they reminded her too much of work so she turned off the main road and found herself in a network of little side-streets. There were silversmiths and jewellers, diamond merchants and galleries and a host of intriguing boutiques. And then she reached the bank of a canal and spent some time looking down into the green water, thinking about Elliot.

It was as if he had produced a magic carpet. She supposed he had wanted someone, anyone, to accompany him today, and perhaps his secretary was too busy to take time off. He had chosen her because he couldn't bear to feel she'd beaten him completely and, as he had said, they were having a sort of truce. What else he had said about her being beautiful was exaggeration, of course, and she was a gullible idiot if she thought it meant anything special. As Rachel she was quite ordinary. Men always looked at girls, didn't they? It meant nothing. To a man like Elliot compliments were his normal stock in trade.

Having got that sorted out in her head, she retraced her steps to be in good time for their twelve o'clock meeting. Despite herself she felt her heart somersault when she saw him already waiting for her. She gave him a beaming smile. 'I've had the most heavenly time,' she exclaimed, despite her darker thoughts of a few minutes ago. 'You must come and have a look at a gallery I found. Do you like paintings?'

He laughed, taking her hand and crumpling it inside his pocket as they went outside to find it. Somehow she mistook the turning and they found themselves walking a leafy path alongside a canal. Houseboats lined the bank.

'It's so beautiful,' she breathed. 'I'd no idea it would be so lovely. Look at the reflections of those trees in the water.'

But Elliot was looking at her. He turned so that they were facing each other and put out his fingers, tracing the gentle curve of her upper lip. She felt her skin tingle. Every touch was an intimation of heaven. Even his hand round her wrist where he still kept it trapped in his pocket seemed like magic, like a bewitchment she only half understood.

He didn't kiss her, but a kiss seemed to hang in the air.

They walked slowly on, his arms wrapped round her shoulders now. Looking like lovers, she thought. In the City of Love. I'm so happy. In a sad way this is as happy as I've ever been.

They had lunch in a small waterside café, sitting in the open at a painted table with the scent of roses coming to them from the vines that tumbled round the balcony of the upper floor. People were talking, soft-voiced, around them, and the aroma of cigars and good coffee floated over the sunlit air. The enchantment of being with Elliot made her feel drowsy—it was like being under a spell, as if nothing else were real.

'Let's see if we can find this little gallery of yours,' he suggested after lunch.

She allowed him to walk her slowly into the network of side-streets. They came across a market selling clogs and brass pots and wooden puppets and he bought her one of those, telling her it was an Indonesian shadow puppet and represented a princess from a Balinese fairy-tale. But his voice was flat when he said, 'Pity you have to go back at eight. We could eat Indonesian-style tonight if we had the time.'

He gave her a curious look as if expecting her to change her mind, his eyes deep clefts of Prussian blue holding the unspoken question.

Confused, she turned away. 'Look,' she cried, darting forward with relief, 'here's the street with the gallery in it!' He hadn't asked why she was in such a hurry to return and, though courtesy suggested that she offer some explanation, she couldn't bring herself to admit something that would change the mood of this idyllic interlude forever.

I'm going to *have* to tell him about Zia, she warned herself as she followed him down some steps into the gallery. But I'll do it later on the way back, she told herself. I'll do it then.

They became too busy arguing about their preferences among the paintings that lined the walls to allow any opportunity for confession, and Rachel was glad when the reasons for her going back at eight seemed to have been dropped. Later, though, another opportunity to tell him about Zia arose when they were passing the opera house. Elliot made quite a show of pointing it out to her.

Then he asked casually, 'Do you sing?'

The question was so unexpected that she gave a gasp and dropped her handbag. It flew open, spilling keys, cards, purse, diary and other oddments all over the pavement. By the time he had helped her pick everything up he seemed to have forgotten the question that had precipitated such a reaction and she hadn't the courage to pursue it. Later, she told herself, I'll tell him when we're sitting down somewhere and can have a quiet talk.

They strolled around for another hour or so until the sun went down and the trees lining the canals began to glimmer in a ghostly fashion through fingers of evening mist.

'We've just time for a drink of hot chocolate before we need to head back towards the airport,' he told her. He led her to a crowded little bar by the waterfront.

'It's been a wonderful day, Elliot,' she said as soon as they were settled in a cosy corner beside a log fire. 'Thank you so much. I shall never forget it.' She meant it in more ways than he could realise and longed to tell him how she felt, but the knowledge that he would see it as a sign that he had broken through her icy defences made her hold her tongue. Besides, she was building up to telling him something far more important.

He gave a distant smile. 'Lovely place, pleasant company.' He laughed shortly. 'We've had it all today, haven't we?'

There was a note of bitterness in his tone despite the words, and she wondered what she had done to make him sound like that. Before she could begin to set things straight he wanted to go, and once outside he stepped into the road to hail a cab. She waited patiently while he spoke to the driver, then he turned back with an odd expression. 'Get in,' he said, 'but don't count on getting back to London before eight. They're cancelling some flights and putting others on hold. I hope this eight o'clock assignation of yours isn't important?'

'What's wrong?' she asked, ignoring the latter part of his question.

'Didn't you pick up on what the driver said? Schiphol's paralysed by fog.' He peered out of the window as the buildings thinned out on the edge of town. It was true. She could see for herself. Fog lay in an unbroken blanket on both sides of the cab. Soon the driver was pulling into the side of the road. Elliot leaned forward to listen to what he had to say. Then the cab was doing a full turn and began to head back to town.

'He says he can't risk it. It's even worse than when he left an hour ago. I guess we'll simply have to stay the night.'

'But I *can't*!' Rachel exclaimed.

Elliot gave her a cynical glance. 'If you have any alternative means of transport at your disposal, do tell me. You can't imagine I'd choose to stay the night here if there were a way out, do you?'

Rachel glowered back at him. It was obvious what he meant. He wouldn't choose a night with Rachel the prude if he had a choice. She glared out of the window.

'It's no use looking like that. Fog, unlike human beings, is impervious to your basilisk stare.'

She sat back and closed her eyes. 'So what do we do?'

'You'll make a phone call to the man you were presumably meeting this evening and then we'll take a room—or should I say rooms?—in a hotel.' He lolled back in a corner of the cab, and when she opened her eyes he was looking directly into them. 'Don't spoil a perfect day, Rachel. You know you can trust me. I gave you my word. And if you think I planned this I only wish I had your faith in my powers. Believe me, this is not the weather I would ordain!'

'Blue skies and golden beaches with lots of bronzed bodies in view would be more your line, I suppose.' She tried to speak lightly but he wasn't fooled.

'Your bronzed body would be enough for me. Provided you were there willingly,' he told her. He was half smiling. 'Stop looking so nervous. We've got a truce on, don't forget.'

'OK.' She smiled.

'Separate rooms sound safe enough, don't they?'

Only if they're in separate buildings too, she wanted to say, but thought it wiser to hold her tongue.

CHAPTER NINE

ELLIOT told the taxi driver to take them back to the centre and they were dropped at the hotel where he had had his early morning meeting. He was obviously known there and he obtained a suite with separate bedrooms without any trouble. Before they went up to see it he suggested going into the hotel's shopping mall to make a few purchases. 'Whatever you need,' he told her, 'toothbrush, nightdress and so on. Charge it to me.'

She felt awkward as she made her few purchases, and when he saw she had confined herself to the bare minimum of toothbrush and toothpaste he raised his eyebrows.

'What about a nightdress?' he asked. 'Or do you usually sleep in the raw?'

She blushed. 'They're all horribly expensive, Elliot. It seems extravagant for just one night.'

'Idiot. Let's see what they've got to offer.'

He forced her back inside the boutique and a sales assistant gushingly showed them a selection of silk nightgowns while Rachel stood to one side, hardly saying a word and letting Elliot do the choosing. When they got outside he handed her the box with a rueful smile. 'You don't seem very enthusiastic. I'm sorry there was nothing there you liked.'

'It's not that!' she burst out. 'They're all simply gorgeous. But it felt wrong for you to buy me something like this. I feel like——' She felt colour flame in her cheeks. 'Well, it was obvious what that assistant thought, wasn't it?'

He lifted his head.

'She thought I was your *mistress*!'

He had started to laugh when he saw how hot and bothered she looked, but when he heard the word 'mistress' his jaw clenched. 'You seem to find the idea offensive,' he rasped. He gave her a freezing glance before saying. 'Better come up and inspect the rooms right away to make sure there's a double lock on your door!' Without giving her chance to protest he grasped her roughly by the arm and insisted on pulling her across the foyer beside him. She had to hurry to keep up so that nobody could guess how tightly he was holding her beneath the folds of her coat. When they reached the stairs he forced her to walk up them rather than take the lift.

'You know I can't be trusted in lifts,' he grated, eyes still glinting. For a moment she thought he was going to give that sudden smile of his to show it was all a joke, but his expression hardened and he didn't say a word all the way up to their suite. When they got inside he thrust her forward into the room.

'Go on, then! Inspect the place. I'd hate you to feel you were being compromised in any way!'

'It—it seems all right,' she said hesitantly, giving the place only the briefest glance. The way he was treating her now told her as plain as day that he had no intention of coming anywhere near her. The realisation wounded her, but she knew it was what she'd asked for. And it was what she wanted, after all.

As if to continue the charade, he poked his head round all the doors and inspected the locks. 'Yes, I think you'll be safe enough here.' He rattled the key in the lock of one of the rooms. 'All right?' he snarled, turning on her.

'I'm sorry, Elliot——'

'Don't apologise, for God's sake. It only makes matters worse. Now you'd better ring this man of yours, hadn't you? Where does he hang out, in a monastery or something?'

'There is no man.' She glanced nervously at the telephone in the window.

'But you hope I'll leave the room so you can phone in private?' He paused as if allowing her the chance to deny it, but when she thought of what she was going to have to say to Ray she dropped her glance. 'Go on, then,' he bit out, 'but make it quick, damn you! I'll be in the bar.' With that he strode from the room.

His face was still white when she joined him a few minutes later after calling Ray to say she wouldn't be in that night.

'I'm intrigued to know what line you gave him,' he grunted when she sat down beside him. 'How did you explain *me* away?'

'I don't have to explain you away to anyone, Elliot,' she began in a small voice. 'Honestly——'

'*"Honestly"*? That's hardly a word I would expect you to use, Rachel.'

She looked at him with incomprehension.

He gave a bitter smile. 'At least you didn't take long to whisper your sweet nothings in his ear. You must be very sure of him.' Before she could hit back he went on, 'Keep it light, that was the pact, wasn't

it? Come on, then. You must be hungry. Let's eat.'
He got up. 'Stay right here while I call a cab.'

When he left she slumped miserably where she
was on the love-seat in the corner of the bar and
wondered why he was so angry with her all of a
sudden. His anger might have flared up when she'd
said she felt like his mistress in the lingerie boutique,
but it had been slumbering beneath the surface long
before that. He had tried to hide it and on the
surface everything had seemed fine. But she had
sensed it was there all the time.

Try as she might, she couldn't imagine what she
had done, apart from not want to get involved in
an affair. And his suspicion that she was ringing
another man to cancel a date was ridiculous. She
hadn't done a thing to lead him to make such an
accusation.

When he came back she tried to be as concili-
atory as possible and skirted any further references
to locked doors or phone calls. He seemed to give
his tacit agreement to a truce between them and
was almost his old self as they made their way out
to the waiting cab.

'I was sorry earlier when I thought we'd have to
miss out on our Indonesian meal,' he told her conversationally. 'If you've never tried it you're in for
a treat.'

It was a tiny restaurant on the upper floor of one
of those tall Dutch houses beside a canal. Outside
was a simple name sign on the austere brick front,
but inside it was a riot of exotic colour. The
rhythmic sound of gamelan music added to the out-
of-this-world feeling as soon as they stepped
through the door. Sitting side by side on braided

cushions, they were soon surrounded by a num-
berless array of little dishes, each bearing a brightly
coloured concoction of exotic-looking food. A
waitress in traditional dress explained what each of
them was, and when she left Elliot picked out his
own favourites for Rachel.

Everything seemed good between them again,
and it was no effort to forget the black clouds on
the horizon. He had said this was a day out of time
and she reminded herself that she had resolved to
live it as if there were no tomorrow. Now, under
the warmth of his glance, she was willing to shut
her eyes to everything else.

She felt her face glow whenever their glances
meshed and she knew that the way his hand re-
peatedly brushed hers as they helped themselves to
the different dishes spread before them was no accident at all. He was responding to her mood and
it made her feel as if for a short spell all the storm
clouds were firmly below the horizon. She refused
to permit herself to imagine what might lie ahead
if their present mood continued. As he had shown
her, there were locks on their doors. It was a
dangerous thought—but she knew that the only
locks she wanted were not ones to keep him out,
but ones to keep him in.

As the evening wore on she realised that now
might be the time to confess to her other role as
Zia, but the intention was quashed by the romantic
ambience of the place, and even though she tried
to make a tentative beginning, whispering. 'I feel
I ought to tell you something, Elliot . . .' he cut her
short at once.

'So solemn, Rachel! Cheer up!' And she remembered their agreement—nothing heavy—and thankfully acquiesced. At this moment everything was too perfect to spoil with a lot of explanations.

To counter any accusation that she was being too serious she searched her mind for something neutral to talk about and blurted, 'Have you been here before?' Then she gave a little laugh. 'Sorry, that's hardly the most original question!'

He chuckled. 'I don't come here often either. Do you?' His eyes teased and he went on, 'I've been saving this place for someone special——' he paused '—then I got impatient.' His tone momentarily hardened, even though he had obviously meant it as a joke, and when her head flew up he added more gently, 'It's said to be the best outside Bali, and it probably is, judging by tonight. Though maybe,' he went on more softly still, 'that impression is something to do with present company...'

In the pause that followed she blushed and looked down at the cloth. 'I suppose you've actually been to Bali?' She couldn't trust herself to remain in control if he continued to look at her like this.

'Once or twice,' he admitted, more conversationally. 'I was on the West Coast for two years, working for a firm of financial consultants. I took every chance I could to travel. Being about halfway to the Far East already, I thought it seemed crazy not to go the whole way...' He laughed and his eyes found hers again, uttering unspoken thoughts that made her nerves tingle.

'It must be lovely,' she replied demurely, trying not to show how her imagination was running wild.

'I can scarcely imagine what it must be like. Different from Dorset, I should think! I'd love to travel,' she added wistfully. 'I've only ever been to Europe.'

Eyes endlessly deep drew forth a response that frightened her in its intensity and, striving to keep the conversation as light as possible, she went on quickly, 'I've had a school skiing trip to Austria, a fortnight in Italy—and an Easter holiday in Spain. I'd like to go to Greece especially,' she added in a rush, feeling that if she kept on talking she could skirt the danger that loomed.

'I'd like to take you to Greece—I mean, I would have liked to——' he corrected. 'Sorry, it's difficult to keep away from the thought that our destinies aren't being woven together. Seems a waste,' he said with a visible effort at lightness, 'when you want to travel and I've done so much and could really show you around. There are so many places I'd like to take you. If we had the time.'

'I like lying on beaches,' she said for something to say. 'I'd like to learn how to windsurf.'

'I could teach you.'

She imagined him, bronzed, muscled, swooping over a sea as blue as his eyes with the gorgeous colours of a sail above him, the slim craft obeying his every command. 'I like old buildings, too,' she said hurriedly. 'Finding out how people used to live.'

'So do I.'

'And looking at paintings——'

'And churches?'

'Yes, and palaces like the ones in Venice.'

'You'd like Thailand.'

'I would?' She knew she'd like anywhere—with Elliot by her side.

'And certainly Greece,' he went on, oblivious to her thoughts. 'I wonder if you'd like the States?'

'I expect so.' Elliot, the mad thought came into her head, shall I tell you what I'm really thinking? But she stifled the question before it could be uttered and instead asked carefully, 'Do you speak a lot of languages?'

'Only French and Italian, but I try to get by as much as possible in the local language. It's only good manners.'

'You seemed to understand the taxi driver.'

'Fortunately.'

She laughed. There was a protracted pause while she dwelt on the intensity of the particular shade of blue of his eyes. There would be a scientific theory to explain it, she didn't doubt. And a special name for the nuances of shade that made them seem like vast oceans, skies of eternity, the colour of heaven itself. They were eyes that seemed to enter the soul. Like a physical penetration.

'Who do you take after in looks?' she blurted.

'Father,' he said at once, 'though he's a thorough-going patriarch now with a mane of white hair. It gets him deferential treatment wherever he goes and he certainly plays up to it.' He spoke affectionately, and she could just imagine the two of them, father and son, their friendly sparring, their banter.

'My mother,' he went on, 'is ash-blonde, like you.'

'Like me?' So that was how he saw her! 'Mouse, you mean, don't you?'

'Not at all.' He cast a judging eye over her hair. 'It's probably what my sister would call baby-blonde. I like it up. She's dark like me,' he went on hurriedly as if not wishing to dwell on what else he liked, but she could see what was in his mind from the way his eyes flicked over her lips.

'You have a sister?' she managed to ask in as near normal a tone as usual.

'Older than me.' He was looking at her as if he was thinking about something entirely different just then. 'We used to fight when we were younger but she's become quite decent now she's more mature.'

'She has? I suppose you were always mature?'

'Naturally.' He laughed. 'What about you?'

'Sisters?' She could scarcely tear her eyes away from his. Her limbs were like molten wax. She tried to pull herself together. 'Two,' she managed to croak, 'both married to farmers. I'm the baby of the family. I've got three older brothers, too. One's a vet, one's a horse-trainer and the third is going to take over the farm when he can eventually persuade Dad he's old enough.'

'How old is he?'

'Thirty-five!'

Elliot chuckled and managed to drag his glance from hers for a second. 'I had the opposite problem,' he resumed. 'I was thrown into the family firm as soon as I left Harvard. I had to take those two years out to prove I could do something on my own account. I've told them I'll knock this place into shape for them, then I'm moving on. Still,' he frowned, 'I won't bore you with shop talk. My folks are well out of it themselves. They winter in Miami and the West Indies and travel around from one house-party to the next for the rest of the year. I told Dad I can't wait to retire!' He suddenly covered her hand with his. 'Listen to us. We're talking like old cronies. I thought we'd be fighting all evening, you sulking in your corner because I'd caused this fog to come down.'

'I don't really sulk——'

'I don't believe you sulk ever—you're much too sparky.'

He smiled when she asked, 'Is that a compliment of some sort?' He looked so warm and inviting that she could have cuddled up to him and put her head on his shoulder. But she knew that the minute the physical gap between them disappeared the surge of animal magnetism would devastate all such chaste intentions. Even so, it was all she could do not to raise her hand and let her fingers trail over the welcoming contours of his lips. She turned away with a small frown. 'What if the fog hangs around all tomorrow?' she asked. 'What will you do?'

'Take you round the Rijksmuseum.'

'No.' She stifled a smile. 'I mean about work?'

'Forget it.'

'Can you?'

'I've done so quite successfully this evening. Being with you——' He broke off. 'What about something else to eat?' he asked in a quite different tone, as if the warmth in his voice just now had been imaginary.

'You must be joking,' she replied more airily than she felt. 'I couldn't eat another morsel. That was simply heavenly.'

'Yes. It was.' He gave a lop-sided smile. 'Quite heavenly, Rachel dear. The stuff of fond mem-

ories?' He quirked an eyebrow, mocking himself
for uttering such pleasantries.

It was late when they eventually set off back to the
hotel. It had been a long and romantic meal. The
best Rachel could ever remember. She was drowsy
now, but with a wonderful sense of well-being.

In the back of the taxi Elliot had held her in his
arms and, though he hadn't kissed her—just as he
hadn't kissed her all day—she could tell his lips were
aching to do just that, as were her own too.

When we get back to the privacy of the hotel,
she told herself with a wild shudder of anticipation, he'll kiss me as he has done before. She
wondered if she would be able to help what happened next.

As soon as they reached the foyer, though, she
was in for a shock. Putting a hand on her shoulder,
he said curtly, 'Go on up. I'm going to have a
nightcap in the bar.'

'Oh? But, what about me?' she asked. 'Don't I
get one too?'

He gave her an amused glance. 'I'll have one sent
up. What do you want?'

'No, I mean, can't I join you?'

'Go up, Rachel, get into bed and go to sleep,' he
said, turning her gently towards the lift. He called
one down for her and saw her safely into it. When
she pulled back he asked, 'You're not bothered
about going up alone, are you? Would you like me
to accompany you?'

'Not if you're going to go back down again by
yourself,' she said, unable to hide her confusion.

He placed a light kiss on her forehead. 'Good-
night. Pleasant dreams. I'll send you something nice
up.'

'Don't bother. I don't want anything, thanks.'

'Sure?'

'Yes... But Elliot——' she protested as the doors
began to close. But they snapped shut, cutting off
her words in mid-sentence.

Puzzled that he should leave her so abruptly, she
wandered round the suite, hoping to hear him come
back, and when she finally decided to get a shower
she listened for the door all the time. But she
climbed out and slipped into the expensive silk
nightdress all without hearing a sound. Eventually,
after a last look round the empty suite, she climbed
into bed, leaving her door ajar and settling down
to wait impatiently for his return.

She must have dozed off, because it was someone
calling her name, her stage-name, that woke her
up.

She opened her eyes and looked round before remembering where she was. The bedside clock said
seven minutes past three. A movement in the adjoining room drew her glance. There was a light
on. After a moment it went out and she heard the
sound of a door closing. He's back, she registered.
She lay for quite a few minutes wondering what
had gone wrong. He must have known from the
way she looked at him in the restaurant that she
had reached the point where she was willing to sacrifice all her inhibitions for him. She had taken him
literally when he'd told her he wanted them to live
for the day. Now it seemed he hadn't meant what

she'd thought he meant after all, otherwise why had he gone to his own room?

She buried her head in the pillow. What if it was his voice that had woken her up, calling out to see if she was still awake? In her sleep she might have mistaken the sound for Zia. Then, realising she was asleep, maybe he had decided not to disturb her? She didn't ask herself why he had taken such a long time to follow her up. It was enough that he had called to her.

No sooner had the thought entered her head than she rose from beneath the duvet. The silk and lace nightdress fell away from her breasts as she slid over the edge of the bed.

Scarcely bothering to rearrange it and without allowing herself to think what she was doing, she let herself drift across the adjoining room until she was standing outside his door. Cautiously, heart thumping like the hoofs of a runaway horse, she pushed it ajar.

A shaft of light from the street furrowed a path through the velvety darkness within. When her eyes became accustomed to the gloom she could make out the pale shape of the bed on the far side. Pace by pace she moved towards it.

She felt so nervous now that she was here, even though he seemed to be asleep, that she reached its side without being able to utter a word. Holding her breath, she knelt down beside the bed and reached out her hands. He really did seem to be asleep, she thought, judging by the evenness of his breathing. Silently she rested her head on his chest.

Nothing happened.

She didn't know what to do next. It was enough for the moment simply to be as close as this. She could sleep like this, she was thinking. Tears of longing filled her eyes. She lifted her head and cautiously pressed kisses against the side of his neck. Then she let her lips move gently along the hard line of his jaw, then they began to seek out the hollows of his cheek, to explore the crevice of his closed eyes, to trail back slowly, warmly, and a little more quickly to the fullness of his lips. She felt him stir as their lips met.

Suddenly one of his hands was trailing through her hair, pressing the hollow at the nape of her neck, caressing her shoulders, and moving lower beneath the silk of her nightdress along the small muscles of her back. His lips sought hers, giving rather than receiving kisses now, his head lifted from the pillow and his other hand searching through the folds of silk for her breasts. Then his fingers were trapping one of her nipples, moving in a way she had never imagined.

With a sharp gasp of pleasure Rachel felt her spine arch, then somehow or other she was being forced back on the bed and he was leaning over her, his hot mouth everywhere, hands and arms entwined as he forced her further and further back. Her bones seemed to melt at his touch. The whole room was one pulsing scarlet flower with their joined bodies at the centre of it, and as soon as her mouth was free she groaned his name in a helpless cry of desire.

He raked her body from scalp to thigh, giving one long, torturing sigh, before she felt his weight shift.

There was a rustling sound as he rolled off the bed. 'Rachel,' he said from across the room a moment later, 'don't bother to explain what your game is. I'm not interested. Would you go...?'

She barely managed to croak her surprise. '*Go?* But *why*?' she asked in breathless astonishment when she succeeded in pulling herself together.

'You know this isn't what you want. You'd be full of recriminations in the morning.'

'I *do* want it, Elliot——' she began.

' "It" possibly. Me, never. Now go. I want some sleep.'

'I didn't mean it like that,' she began heatedly, mortified beyond all limits by her own careless words.

'I'm really not interested in what you did or did not mean.' He pretended to yawn. She could see the outline of his head against the white wall.

'If you were really tired you'd have come to bed earlier,' she bit out. 'What's gone wrong? Why are you pretending?'

'I might ask you the same thing.' He stayed where he was but she could feel his eyes piercing the darkness as if to scour her expression.

'I'm not pretending, Elliot, I'm really not. I *do* want you, I *do*. I should know! I've wanted you all evening...in the restaurant, when you touched my hand, when you seemed to respond——'

He gave a harsh laugh. 'I'm not made of stone. What did you expect me to do when you look so seductive? I'm sorry if I made you think it meant anything else. Now, for the last time, will you leave me in peace?'

'Elliot! You can't mean this!' She knew she was losing all sense of shame, but it was dark and she was pushed to say things she would never dare say in the broad light of day. Tomorrow didn't matter. She had decided to shut her eyes to it. Without planning it she jumped down off the bed and ran across the room, catching hold of his arm and slipping the other one around his neck in an impulsive gesture that outflanked his resistance for a moment, 'Elliot, I'm sorry I've been so un——' she floundered for the right word '——uncooperative——'

He gave a grunt of anger and moved away. 'I don't want "co-operation", Rachel,' he muttered hoarsely. 'I want what you're patently incapable of giving, and that's a genuine response. And don't do that——' He gave a groan and buried his head in her hair. *'Stop it,'* he rasped, 'or I won't be responsible for the consequences!'

She had innocently pressed her body against his and was shocked to feel the evidence of his arousal. It left her in no doubt that he wanted her despite his words. 'Elliot . . .' she murmured, reaching up for his mouth.

There was a breathless moment when he plunged his tongue deep inside as his arms came round her, gripping her tightly against his pulsing body. He tensed, and for one swooning second she felt the primitive urgings of desire take possession of them both before his engulfing kiss turned to something more primitive still. A sort of primal savagery took over. Her mouth felt plundered and she tried to fight him off. But he held her even more tightly and she heard the fine silk of her gown rasp along her thighs as he dragged it to her waist.

With an abruptness that was unexplained he jerked away, releasing his hold on her so that she staggered back in a billow of silk, almost sinking to her knees on the deep-pile carpet. He shot out a hand to jerk her to her feet, then pushed her away as soon as she stumbled close again.

'I said *get out*!' he snarled. He crossed the room to the door and opened it. *'Please.'* His voice was like the grating of ice on ice, and the fact that he didn't use her name made it sound colder still.

'I don't understand,' she breathed raggedly. Too distraught for anger or grief, she could only stand there in the darkness, twisting her hands together.

'There's nothing much to understand, is there? From your point of view, that is. You made your wishes clear before we got here. I'm not going to be responsible for the whims of the night. As far as I'm concerned everything is as it was when I invited you to come over here. Let's forget this ever happened and try to get a good night's sleep. All right?'

'Is that some sort of olive branch, Elliot? I suppose it is,' she went on before he could answer. 'I'm sorry,' she whispered as she walked past him. She felt about two inches high. It was bad enough to have thrown herself at a man, any man, something she had never done before. But for it to be the man she loved, when he didn't even know it, and to be rejected so unambiguously by him, was the worst thing she could imagine. She felt as if she had been through a mangle and had just come out the other side.

She heard him close the door behind her. Seeking the solitude of her own room, she lay down on the bed, knowing she would be awake for the rest of what remained of the night.

CHAPTER TEN

FEELING somewhat shamefaced when she met Elliot next morning, Rachel was grateful when he made no direct reference to the previous night other than to comment on how surprisingly rested she looked. As if to disprove him, on the flight home her intention to admit to Zia's existence just to clear the slate was thwarted by the simple fact that she fell asleep at once. Only when she felt a hand on her shoulder did she open her eyes. She shook her head, looking round. The plane had already come to a standstill.

'It's a shame to wake you. You make me feel like a cad,' he said huskily, 'but I guess there'd be trouble with the maintenance staff if you tried to stay on board now we've landed!'

'Heavens, I'm so sorry! I must have fallen asleep straight away!' Rachel sat upright, trying to collect her thoughts. 'Is it really London again?' Rain was pouring out of an overcast sky made darker still by the fact that it was already past midday.

'Put my raincoat over your head, we'll run for it,' he suggested. 'Ready?'

They splashed through the puddles to the shelter of the arrival lounge, laughing and breathless, for a moment all antagonism forgotten. Elliot spun her into his arms, his black hair dripping with moisture, little beads of rain standing out on the end of his eyelashes, his skin wind-whipped.

For a moment Rachel's breath was stopped by the feeling of love for him that surged over her. Her eyes half closed as he bent to kiss her cheek. What had been intended as a light kiss turned suddenly into something fierce, suggesting emotion held too long in check. Their bodies sought and found each other, clinging with a possessiveness that left them both breathless.

Other travellers were beginning to notice them. 'I'll get you a taxi,' he muttered hoarsely, dragging her out after him. On the concourse he held her close again as if suddenly reluctant to let her go, his mouth searching for hers with an unexpected force that took her completely by surprise. Why had he sent her away last night if he really wanted to kiss her? He had behaved as if he couldn't bear to have anything to do with her. She didn't understand.

But she willingly reached out to him now, returning kiss for kiss, senses aching with the need to hold nothing back. This is the last time, she kept telling herself as her lips sought his. The last time for all time. She allowed him to possess her lips as if she could convey all her longing for him, her desire for him to take all of her, in their mere touch, and it was only her hoarsely whispered name that brought her reeling back to the present.

His eyes were a blaze of harsh blue, sweeping her with an appraising expression. Was it with triumph that he stepped back? She felt crushed by the abrupt change in him, wanting to cry out, *Don't let it end,* but he was already retreating, moving back across the footway, his intention to call a cab uppermost again.

Wordlessly she watched as one pulled into the kerb. She allowed herself to be put inside, expecting, half hoping, that he would get in beside her. But instead he slammed the door, standing for a second with his hand on it looking in at her. Then with a strange twist of a smile he raised one hand in farewell. The cab began to slide away. He was looking down the road after it. When she turned her head to peer through the rear window he was in the same position, head inclined, as he watched it gather speed and disappear from view.

He wasn't in the club that night. Deflated, Rachel kicked off her shoes and began to peel away the make-up as soon as she came off stage. She couldn't face Henry tonight. For some reason she ached all over, as if heartache had spread to every fibre of her body. Ray looked in and immediately called a cab.

'Your six weeks is nearly up, Rachel. Do you know what you're going to do?' he said when he came back and she was dressed ready to leave.

She shook her head. 'Herman hasn't been in touch. I hope everything's all right. I signed the contract. But I've heard nothing since; I don't know whether he's been able to get me work or not.'

Ray merely nodded. 'I'll call him in the morning and drop a hint or two. I'd like you to stay—if there's nothing immediately we can renew the arrangement informally week by week. But if he's got anything better lined up for you, you should take it.'

At that moment Rachel felt she didn't give a damn. Was this, she asked herself, what dedication meant? Endless pain? Endless loneliness? Heartbreak?

It was a luxury not to have to be on the Tube at eight-fifteen every morning to get into the store on time. The first couple of days after she left she stayed in bed. Sleeping. Sleeping her pain away, she told herself, and thought it had worked until she emerged and glimpsed a figure in the street who for a brief moment looked like Elliot, making her heart leap into her mouth—and she knew she wasn't over him at all.

I *will* forget in time, she told herself. I'll have to if I'm going to survive. But there was an unexpected ordeal ahead.

Because he hadn't put in an appearance at the club she had been lulled into believing he was out of her life for good. It was illogical to imagine a connection between the two absences—he himself couldn't connect Rachel with Zia so would have no reason for avoiding the Manhattan if he wanted to avoid Rachel as he so obviously did. But she got it into her mind that for some reason she would never have to set eyes on him again. However, it was not to be so easy.

A week later, looking tanned and if possible even more handsome than usual, he came strolling into the club around midnight, just as she had launched into a sentimental ballad from one of the latest shows.

'"No love like ours can die——"' she sang, then the words seemed to freeze in her throat as she caught sight of him standing on the edge of the darkened dance floor by himself. Pulling herself

together she went on, ' "Our love is forever, I know
it's true...'cos loving you...is all I ever want..." '
The words were trite, but she couldn't stop herself
from singing them as if they meant everything in
the world. And with Elliot standing so close, they
did.

When the last note died she quickly left the stage.
His sudden appearance was like a blow to the
stomach. But before she had chance to kick off her
stilettos there was a loud rapping on the dressing-
room door. She moved towards it like someone in
a dream.

'Hi!' He draped himself in the doorway and
made no move to come inside. Even guessing who
would be standing there hadn't prepared her for
the jolt to her senses when she found them both
face to face with only inches between them.

'Hi,' she managed to croak. 'Long time no see...'
She backed into the room but didn't invite him to
follow. He seemed quite content to stay where he
was.

'You're looking as delectable as ever, Zia. Things
are obviously going well.' His lips seemed to twist
rather derisively.

'You're looking pretty good yourself,' she
managed to stammer. 'Life's treating you all right?'

'Everything's absolutely wonderful,' he agreed.
'Not a cloud in the sky.' He eyed her without
speaking and she could feel his glance trail rapidly
over her shape in the revealing black gown before
coming back to rest on her face.

'You look well,' she managed to say, trying to
ignore the urge to reach out and touch him. The
tan he had acquired suited him. He had obviously

got over Rachel in double-quick time to be going off on holiday. There must have been plenty of beach life to help take his mind off her! 'Been somewhere nice?' she asked in tones casual enough to disguise the rapid beating of her heart.

He shook his head. 'Too much work here to take time off,' he told her.

She gave him a disbelieving glance. 'You're very tanned,' she remarked critically.

'My health club solarium, I'm afraid. Did you think I'd been away?'

She nodded.

'I'm surprised you noticed.'

She bit her lip. 'Well——' she shrugged naked shoulders '—you were becoming a fixture here. Naturally I noticed.' She tried to sound flippant. 'I thought maybe you'd gone off my singing...I know you prefer——' she half smiled '—something a little heavier.'

'Opera, you mean?'

She nodded.

'Funny you should mention that,' he went on smoothly. 'I was going to ask you if you'd like to accompany me to a performance of *Madama Butterfly*? I happen to have a box.' There was a long pause.

Rachel found herself reaching for the back of a chair. Everything told her to say no at once—she had already played with fire and was still suffering the burns. But before she could stop herself she found herself nodding in agreement. 'I'd love to,' she heard herself say. 'I adore Puccini.'

If he was surprised by her response he didn't show it, but merely made arrangements to meet then left.

What have I done? was Rachel's first thought as the door closed behind him. Then she pulled herself together. The reason was obvious. It hadn't felt right to go on hiding her true identity from him, despite the fact that there was no future for them together. Now she would have a perfect opportunity to tell him the truth.

She had never liked the deception, for that was what it had unwittingly turned into. He had looked puzzled and hurt by her reticence about her life outside the store during their brief sojourn in Amsterdam. He had told her a lot about himself, about his school, his boyhood, his mother and father, touching briefly also on his business course at Harvard, his two years with an American company on the West Coast. She treasured every word, but even though she had longed to share her inmost secrets she had been unable to offer much in return. She hadn't started living until she came to London, and the only important thing she had done since was the one thing she was unable to confess.

The next evening Lulu happened to call to see her on her way home from work. For once Ros was in and Rachel introduced the two of them. Afterwards Ros looked rather disapproving. 'I'm not surprised you've become so fashion-conscious yourself, Rachel. That get-up of hers! Honestly! And you're not seriously going to the opera in a hairpiece as if you're singing at the club, are you?'

Rachel had told Lulu about Elliot's invitation to the opera and she had immediately clapped her hands. 'Now you can put the record straight!' She went on, 'My brother happens to be an opera buff. I'll get the libretto from him then you won't go making a fool of yourself.'

'Actually I do happen to know the story of *Madama Butterfly*. I thought everybody did.' She frowned. 'It's a real tear-jerker...'

'Better wear waterproof mascara, then!' Lulu got up to go. 'I'm *so* glad, Rachel. You deserve a second chance.'

At the door Rachel said, 'It's not a second chance to start things up again. I still think we made the right decision. He's not for me, Lulu. I couldn't handle a relationship with him, I really couldn't. He's out of my league on every level.' Even to Lulu she couldn't confess how deep the heartbreak would be if she risked giving herself to Elliot only to have to face the break later, after they'd become lovers. She was perversely grateful that he had rejected her that night at the hotel, whatever his reasons. Life was unbearable now, but it could have been an even worse hell.

A couple of days later Lulu was back, armed with hot combs, gels and hair sprays to help Rachel transform herself into Zia. After what seemed an age she finally pronounced her ready.

'You look fantastic. Cool, chic, with just a hint of wildness. Darling Elliot will find you utterly irresistible!'

Rachel was a bundle of nerves, and despite Lulu's verdict and even the cautious approval of Ros she would gladly have given the evening a miss. But the toot of the taxi from outside the window came all too soon.

'Thanks for your help, you two.' With a bravado she didn't feel, Rachel moved breathlessly towards the door.

'Good luck, Zia!' called Lulu. 'Give him a peck on the cheek from me!'

CHAPTER ELEVEN

IF HE asked me now whether I can sing or not, Rachel told herself, the answer would be no. She had been enchanted by the performance ever since she heard the first thrilling notes. She closed her eyes as the aria came to an end and for a moment imagined herself happy.

There was a warm breath on her cheek. 'Heaven, isn't it?' whispered a voice in her ear. It was Elliot. There were three of his business colleagues in the box with them.

Rachel turned towards him. His mouth was only inches from her own. 'This is such bliss,' she whispered back. Her voice shook.

He would never know what heaven it was to be beside him. Yet the pain of shutting him out of her life only made her ambition to succeed more important. Sacrifice and dedication went hand in hand. To be a professional singer was something she had been born for. It was a fierce hunger, one she longed to share with someone. But only Elliot could have been the confidant who could have shared her ambitions, and there was no way this could come about, for he was the very person she was being forced to sacrifice. Even as she saw all this, she wondered what would happen if he lifted a finger. Would she go running to him?

She turned her attention back to what was happening on stage. He had treated her with a kind of ironic politeness when he'd met her in the theatre bar before the curtain went up. When they had taken their seats, the stalls below had been a sea of eyes turned in their direction. Whispers went round asking who they were. Rachel would have blushed, while Zia would have gloried in it except for the matter of a broken heart.

So far she hadn't had the chance to talk to Elliot properly, and she decided that it would be best to wait until they were alone after the performance. Then she would be able to reveal her true identity in private. There was no kowing how he would react.

During the interval she caught sight of them both in a faceted wall-mirror surrounded by red plush. They certainly made a handsome couple. Yet when Elliot's glance kept straying to the *décolletage* of her gown she knew exactly what he was thinking of Zia the cabaret singer in this milieu.

'I hardly dare call myself a singer after this,' she admitted, wishing he wouldn't look at her like that.

Unexpectedly he said, 'Don't run yourself down. Yours is a different but no less enviable talent.' Then he half smiled and she wondered if there had been an ambiguity in his compliment after all.

His eyes were on her again and it felt like a finger stroking intimately over every exposed inch of her bosom. Instead of recoiling she felt herself arch provocatively, and the tip of her tongue glossed her lower lip out of sheer nervousness at what his look foretold.

He gave a soft laugh. 'You understand me so well, Zia.' She felt his hand brush the back of hers where it was hidden among the folds of her scarlet satin gown. He went on, 'We could be so good together. Your charms are the most exciting thing about this evening—and I'm in raptures over the production, so you can guess what sort of effect you're having on my—how shall we say?' He paused suggestively. 'Libido?'

She gazed up at him from beneath the layers of false eyelashes, knowing her eyes were shadowed, hoping he couldn't read the despair at this travesty of the love-talk she longed to hear that must surely be mirrored in their depths.

'Do you really mean that, Elliot? I mean, do you think you know me well enough to say such a thing?'

He took her response as a challenge. 'Give me the chance and I'll prove it.' He drew his lips back in a narrow smile. 'Now, tonight.'

There had been talk of going on to dinner with Elliot's colleagues and when she pointed this out he replied, 'Trust me, my dear.' It reminded her painfully of the time in Amsterdam when he had told her that very same thing. She gave a shudder.

'Elliot, I don't think——' she began, but he had turned to join in the general conversation. She knew beyond any shadow of a doubt that it was not the end of the matter.

She watched him playing the urbane host. Obviously he had felt little for Rachel, and her heartache seemed a lonely thing when she saw how one-sided it had been. Her intuition in those early days had been right. He was just another heart-breaker, clever with the sort of love-talk that only an innocent fool like Rachel would have fallen for.

It was as they were making their way back to the box after the second interval that she found herself by chance trailing behind the others. Elliot was by her side. Unseen by anyone, he ran his fingertips down her spine. She responded without being able to stop herself.

Elliot's smile told her he had seen her shiver of pleasure. 'Slow down a little.' He leaned against her, forcing her to a stop halfway up the narrow stairs leading into the ante-room to the box.

'Really Elliot, I don't think——'

'Let them go on ahead.'

Helplessly she saw the green and gilt door close behind them. Then with calculated speed he pushed her into an alcove hung with velvet curtains. They heard the door at the top of the stairs open and a voice saying, 'Where are they?' The reply was cut off when the door closed again.

'Elliot, please——'

'You've been promising so much ever since we met—isn't it about time I collected something on account?' He pushed his face close to hers, dragging her hips hard against his own, and Rachel gave a gasp of surprise as she felt his body's hardness pressing so powerfully against the yielding softness of her own. She felt as weak as a kitten, totally unable to resist. She wasn't Zia, she was Rachel, and this was the man she loved.

'I mustn't——' she managed to gasp as his lips hovered over her own.

'Mustn't?'

'Mustn't weaken——' Her breath was deep and ragged. 'I don't want involvement.'

'I'm not offering involvement. Just a little tender loving.'

'I have a rule, Elliot. *No*——' she protested as his hands started to thrill over her.

'Rule?' he interrupted before she could go on. 'Who's interested in rules? There's only one rule and the rule is love. Now love me the way only you can. The way you sing about.'

'That's only a cabaret act——'

'You mean you don't love like that in real life? But the words are so sexy and you have that certain look in your eye. It signals to every man in the audience that you really know what's what——' He asked brutally, 'You mean to say it's all a sham?' He gave a cynical laugh. 'Don't expect me to believe that. There's no way you could put it over so sexily if you weren't a very experienced young woman. Now stop teasing and kiss me the way I want——'

'I can't, Elliot! Please! Let me go!'

'Certainly not. You're driving me wild, and you know it!' As if to prove it he began to caress her breasts beneath the slithery satin gown, quickly finding the long back zip and to Rachel's horror sliding it rapidly down as far as it would go. The encasing satin fell away like the petals of a scarlet flower and her breasts were revealed, pearly against the blood-red sheen of the gown.

'*No!*' she cried in horror at this outrage as his eyes raked her nakedness with a murmur of desire at what he saw. He gave a deeper groan.

'I want you, woman. Let's get out of here. I'm taking you back to my apartment. Now!' He bent to kiss her breasts.

'No, Elliot!'

'It's around the corner in the piazza in Covent Garden,' he said thickly. 'Just a few steps to heaven, that's all.' He was still kissing her but thankfully, in his haste to get away to somewhere more private, was already beginning to refasten her zip. She felt once that was done up again she would be able to talk him out of this wild scheme, but an image of the undisturbed hours they might spend together flashed before her eyes, taunting her with forbidden fantasies. His hands on her body. Her helpless submission in the arms of the man she loved...

She tried to twist out of his grasp, 'Elliot, please let me go!'

'Never!'

'But your friends! The opera! It's starting again!'

'Damn them and damn the opera! How can you think of opera at a time like this?' he rasped. He pulled her feverishly against him once more, the zip half fastened. 'Make love to me, honey, come on, you know you want to...' He blazed a fiery trail of kisses down the side of her neck. 'Kiss me, I want to feel your lips, your tongue...'

'No, I——' Rachel, breath ragged, was straining back out of his arms, but for all the good it did she could have stayed in them. Their limbs became entwined, every pulsing beat of their hearts echoing one with the other.

'I said kiss me,' he muttered hoarsely. 'You know how to.'

'I don't—I——' But his lips claimed hers in a kiss that surprised her with its tenderness. His mouth was as sweet as honey, persuading her to yield, not forcing her at all. She felt his hand holding her in the small of her back while the other came up to press her head against his shoulder, stroking her hair, pressing her cheek as if to learn its secret structure beneath his palm.

'You're driving me wild, do you know that?' he whispered against her ear. 'Yet when I allow myself to think about it I'm filled with such blind rage... Holding you in my arms like this, I can almost forgive and forget. Then the thoughts come back. The hurt. Why did you think you could lie to me, Rachel? What was the purpose of it?'

'*Rachel?*' She tilted her head back and looked into his eyes. 'You *know*?' She was stunned.

'It's a brilliant disguise and I certainly didn't guess that sex-siren on stage was sweet, demure little Rachel from the store until I met you off stage. Only then did something fail to jell. My suspicions grew. Even so I had a niggling doubt, a doubt which lasted until you dropped your shoulder-bag in Amsterdam... When I helped pick up your things I saw your pass card from the club with the name Zia on it. I couldn't believe it. But it made sense—— ' He shrugged. 'It explained why I had to keep on going back to that place. I guess I really knew it was you all along. Kissing you proved it. I would know your lips anywhere. One kiss and there could be no pretence.'

His face was darkening as seconds ticked by and she went on staring up at him with no apology or explanation. '*Why*, Rachel?' he prompted. 'Did you just want to make a fool of me?'

His look of hurt sent ice up and down her spine. Mutely she shook her head. When he was scarcely able to contain his anger with her like this it seemed to strike her dumb. She could offer no words to explain. No apologies for the hurt. Hurt? she thought helplessly. I'm the one who's hurt—who will be hurt if I succumb to the passion of a one-night affair with a heartbreaker like you. But she could not express her fears to him. It was impossible to say the right words.

'Tell me why you did it, for God's sake!' He lifted a hand, grasping her roughly by the chin. 'Did you girls cook it up between you? Couldn't you see how I felt about you? Have you only a block of ice where other women have a heart?' He was keeping up a rhythmic caressing over the small bones of her back that was numbing all ability to reason.

'Don't, Elliot——' She tried to move away but felt him draw her back.

'I suppose you thought it amusing to play at being sweet Rachel and let me say all those ridiculous things about milkmaids and innocence. My God, how you must have been laughing up your sleeve!' He took hold of a fistful of the false hair that swirled to her shoulders and held it as if liking nothing better than to break her neck. With her dress half undone and her breasts partly exposed she knew she must look as wanton as he imagined her to be. She tried to squirm free, but he hadn't finished yet.

'I'm not going to let you go. You've played with me. Now I'm going to play with you.' He gave a harsh laugh. 'I'm going to have my fill of those tasty lips of yours. Why not? You've flaunted yourself often enough; now you'll have to learn to take what's coming to you!'

He began to draw her in towards him with taunting deliberation. One hand was already sliding inside the gaping bodice while the other held her powerfully around her tiny waist. He could nearly get his hand around it, a fact he commented on with satisfaction.

'And now, Rachel, Zia—my lovely liar, I'm going to kiss you in a way even you've never imagined.'

The faint sound of violins as the orchestra reached a momentary climax came through the door at the top of the stairs. The sound enveloped them in its lyrical beauty, the passionate notes of the lead singers as they joined in echoing the passion that was driving her into Elliot's arms. With no will to resist despite the threat in what he had just said to her, Rachel allowed him to bestow kiss after kiss upon her.

At once she realised it was the worst thing she could do. It merely confirmed what he had just said about her, and when he lifted his head, as well as the blurred look of unassuaged desire, his pride forced a harsh laugh from between his lips.

'Long live Zia. If that's a taste of things to come, what are we waiting for?' He made as if to drag her down the stairs but she pulled back, grappling with the front of her dress at the same time.

Shame at what he thought scorched her cheeks. 'It's not true, Elliot! Only with you——' she cried breathlessly. 'No one else could ever make me feel like this!'

'I'm sure you say that to all your men.'

'Don't be so hateful! I'm not like this!'

'Like what? Wild and wanton? Oh, but you are, Zia. You're very much like this. You're just a naughty little girl playing at being a woman but it still means only one thing—you want to be taken to bed. Look how you behaved in Amsterdam! You were utterly, deliciously, torturingly available!'

Her cheeks flamed.

'I should have taken you then,' he rasped. 'Unfortunately I still believed in Rachel! More fool me!' He shot out a hand to haul her against him. 'Don't pretend you don't want me to take you to bed right now!'

Her lips refused to deny it.

'No, I thought not. One look at your face and what you want is as plain as day. You can't disguise the truth from me any longer. I know you now as well as I know myself!'

'You don't. You think you do, but you don't! I've never—— ' She glanced wildly round but his bulk seemed to block all avenue of escape, asserting the story he believed, making her feel dominated by it, unable to resist his accusations. How could she explain that it was love she wanted; not a fling, not just his body, but his love and respect and a lifetime together? She put a hand up to her mouth. Had she forgotten her ambitions already, merely because he was holding her in his arms?

'Come.' He slid his fingers round her wrist. 'Maybe you're being sensible for once. Let's go back to the box. We have the whole night ahead of us. And Zia...tidy yourself a little.' He reached for her, holding her unnecessarily close. 'Let me fasten your gown.' He kissed the skin beneath the fabric before bringing the zipper up again.

'We're going back?' she asked, confused by his touch as much as by his change of plan.

'I always believe, darling Zia, that things waited for are best. Don't you?'

Rachel felt an overwhelming relief. He had pushed her to the limit of her resistance and she had made a poor showing. If he had pushed just that little bit more she feared she would have been unable to make that final effort. Now, with time in which to gather her resistance, she felt a flicker of hope. Later she would be ready. She would resist. She would say no emphatically, despite the mind-shaking heaven of his touch. But there would be no later, for she would leave as soon as the performance was over even if she had to run from the theatre with the entire audience at her heels.

When they slid into their seats Rachel's eyes sought the bright oblong of the stage. Shaking, she folded her hands in her lap lest Elliot slip her hand into his, and then she tried to concentrate on what was happening beyond the intimate darkness of the box.

At the end, as the heroine lay dying, there wasn't a dry eye in the house, and as far as Rachel was concerned the heartache of the lovers on stage mirrored her own plight with regard to Elliot. But *she* couldn't give up in a paean of glorious song. This was real life and she had to go on. What was more, she had to go on to triumph. It was the only way to give the heartbreak any meaning.

When Elliot suggested going back to his club to have dinner she began by pleading tiredness and begged to be taken home. Surprisingly, he agreed. With a mocking smile he said, 'It's been a remarkable evening, Zia,' and went on loudly enough for everyone to hear, 'I'm not surprised you're emotionally exhausted. You know we'll meet again . . . very soon.'

He must have read the silent vow in her eyes, for as he put her in a taxi he squeezed her waist. 'By now,' he said, 'you should know I always keep my word . . .'

It was Wednesday again and she was due at the Manhattan that evening. When she came in the waiters were bustling about under the main lights, the ones that were never put on during opening times. They seemed to drain all colour from the furnishings, showing the place in its worst, most tawdry aspect. Rachel paused on the threshold. Herman claimed he was working on obtaining a booking for her in a similar kind of place in Spain, but she was beginning to think this was not the kind of environment in which she wanted to continue.

Attending the opera had crystallised something for her and she felt now she wanted to set her sights on a part in a musical show of some kind. Herman had told her to leave it with him. He had, he said, his ear to the ground.

She greeted Ray as usual and was about to go on to ready herself when he called her through into his office.

'I've got something to tell you, Rachel. Take a seat.'

She sat.

'It's this bother with the wife's health,' he told her. 'I've decided to take the plunge. The plunge into retirement, that is. I'm selling up. We're going to the villa on the Costa. It's for the best. No good going on until—well.' He spread his hands. 'I wanted you to know because you might be worried about your job...'

Rachel bit her lip. It looked bad from her point of view, but on the other hand it left her with no alternative but to seek work elsewhere. The more she considered it, the more she realised it would be a relief to get away from a place that reminded her so much of Elliot. Herman would just have to pull his finger out and get her something else. Then Ray said something that took her completely by surprise.

'I have, as it happens, already had an offer for the place. But before I go ahead there is something you need to know. It's this. The prospective purchaser only wishes to proceed on condition that you remain as *chanteuse*.'

Her first reaction was relief. At least she was going to be in work. Then she floundered as she imagined what it would be like to continue in a place that contained so many torturing memories. Stifling such thoughts, she assumed a businesslike manner. 'That must mean my contract is going to be renewed. Presumably under the same terms?'

'You'll have to ask Herman that, my dear. I'm sure he'll do his very best for you.'

Next morning she was on to Herman first thing. 'What is this?' she demanded. Being tough and businesslike had the bonus of keeping thoughts of Elliot at bay.

'Good news, isn't it?' replied Herman genially.

'I'm not sure.'

'He's increasing your salary. That can't be bad.'

'I suppose not,' she admitted. 'But you know I was hoping to start doing a few auditions for shows instead of concentrating on club work.'

She heard Herman say something to someone else in the office with his hand partly covering the mouthpiece. When he came back to her he said, 'There was an audition lined up for you. But if you got the job you'd have to break your contract with the Manhattan.'

'As I haven't signed a contract with the new owner that's not an issue at present, is it?'

When there was another long pause she said, 'Look, Herman, surely you can think of some compromise? I don't want to jeopardise Ray's sale but——' she hesitated '—I do need to broaden my range. And I need that audition for the experience if nothing else.' Of course she didn't go into all her reasons for wanting out.

'You're right,' he agreed, coming to a sudden decision. 'We'll cross our bridges when we get to them as far as the contract goes. If you sign it you'll at least have a job, and then if you get offered something else we'll get out of it somehow. I'll ask my secretary to ring you back with the audition info.'

Things moved swiftly after that. The purchaser, under the name of Stateside Entertainment, began to go ahead in earnest once Rachel signed their contract. At the same time she found herself in a long line of other hopefuls auditioning for a part in a new as yet untitled musical due to open before Christmas.

After the audition she walked into Ray's office with a smile on her face, feeling her spirits lighter than they had been since the night at the opera with Elliot. 'They've asked me to go back, Ray, isn't that wonderful——?' Then the smile froze on her lips.

Elliot, looking more handsome than ever, un-coiled from Ray's swivel chair and leaned on the desk. Ray, in overcoat and grey trilby, stood by the door.

'Just in time!' he said cheerfully. 'Meet the director of Stateside—though I know you know each other,' he added in an aside.

'*What?*' Rachel gulped and stepped back.

Elliot smiled grimly. 'We know each other all right, don't we, Zia?' He came round the edge of the desk, one hand outstretched. 'You've just missed the handing-over ceremony. Welcome to the New Manhattan. May our partnership be mutually satisfying.'

There was no mistaking the double edge to his words. Rachel drew herself up. 'I've just come from an audition,' she began. 'And——'

'I'm sorry?' He looked from Ray to Rachel and back again. 'Has there been some confusion over the terms of the contract, Ray? I don't expect her to be looking for work elsewhere until *I've* finished with her. And that,' he added in a voice full of menace, 'won't be for quite a time.'

CHAPTER TWELVE

AFTER Ray said goodbye and left, Rachel turned on Elliot with a muffled cry. *'You!'* she exclaimed. 'Is it true? It must be some kind of joke!'

'I assure you, my dear, my bank take it very seriously.'

'Your bank?' She frowned.

His glance assessed their surroundings. 'This is an expensive little place, bang in the middle of the West End. It costs. But I'm sure it's going to be worth every penny.'

'But you don't know anything about night-clubs,' she accused.

'Don't I?'

'Maybe you do,' she mumbled, turning away. 'How the hell would I know?' She spun to face him again, her hands twisting helplessly in front of her. 'What made you do it, Elliot?' Already the ramifications were beginning to explode in her mind like so many fire-bombs.

'I thought it an amusing thing to do. You didn't imagine I was happy being a mere shopkeeper, did you?'

The store was one of the most prestigious of its kind and Rachel would have smiled at any other time to hear it referred to as a shop, but now she was too frightened to smile. 'What about me?' she managed to blurt. 'Are you going to tear up my contract?' The thought that she might soon be without a job was at the back of her mind. Even though she had been short-listed for the musical she knew she couldn't count on that. Uppermost though was the realisation that his answer would depend on whether he wanted her around—in any capacity—or not.

Elliot watched her closely as she turned to look at him. 'Tear it up?' he said after an agonising pause. 'I don't think so. Why should I? After all, when I bought the club—I bought you with it.'

Now her heart swooped painfully. '*Bought* me?' She summoned up a scornful glance. 'I'm not for sale, Elliot,' she said through tight lips.

'That's true—now,' he told her coolly. 'But you were for sale, as I've just demonstrated.'

'*I*——' she went right up to him '—*I*,' she repeated, 'am *not* for sale. And never will be!'

'Everyone has their price. *Yours* is clearly stated in the contract. Would you like to back out of it?' Before she could answer he went on, 'Because if so let me know and I'll get on to my solicitors right away.' He gave a sardonic smile. 'There are penalties for breach of contract as I'm sure you know.'

'Elliot, why are you treating me like this?' There was a note of uncertainty in her voice.

'Don't play the innocent, blinking your wide blue eyes like that, Zia.' He uttered her stage name with such sarcasm it was like a slap in the face. 'I'm not taken in any more. You can't get away with playing the innocent Rachel any longer. I've seen through that one, darling. Now, shall we get down to business?'

'I don't know what you mean.' She bowed her head, bewildered by the turn of events and confused further by the genuine dislike Elliot was displaying. Had she hurt his feelings so much? Didn't he see it hadn't been her intention to make him look a fool?

'Elliot, please let me explain——'

'No time for that. You should surely be getting ready to go on?' He glanced at his watch. 'I seem to remember you start at ten-thirty?'

She nodded.

He turned back to some papers on his desk and with a feeling that she was living in some kind of nasty dream she made her way to the sanctuary of her dressing-room.

What now? she thought as she got ready. She resented the suggestion that she had been bought—as if she were part of the fixtures and fittings of the club, she thought bitterly. Who did he think he was? And why, why in heaven's name, had he done it? It all seemed to hint at something but she couldn't guess what.

When she came off around midnight the applause rang hollowly in her ears and she slumped down in her chair, apparent physical exhaustion masking what was really a deep-seated emotional fatigue.

It had all seemed so simple to begin with. Dedication to her career. But that was when she was a complete beginner in life, before she learned even the first letter in the alphabet.

There was a knock on the door and she called out in a weary voice. It would be Piers with Henry's champagne and the inevitable red rose.

'Thank you, Piers, I——' She broke off. Elliot stood there, a rage in his eyes. Behind him she could see the waiter's anxious face.

'What the hell is this?' snarled Elliot. He turned to indicate the waiter and the tray bearing Henry's tokens of esteem.

'As you can see——' She yawned, unable to stop herself.

He swivelled to the waiting Piers. 'Take it all back and tell him——' He stopped. 'No, better not tell a customer what I was just about to say. Tell him "not tonight". Go on.' Piers left and Elliot turned back. 'Does he do that often?'

'Every night, I'm afraid.'

He came inside and closed the door. 'Why don't you tell him to stop?'

'Why should I?' She regarded him levelly in the mirror. His face hovered over her left shoulder.

'You'll tell him it's got to stop.'

It made no odds to her. She had already suggested to Henry that he shouldn't do it but his reply had been that it was a bit of nonsense he enjoyed. Now Elliot's stark order made her anger rise. 'If it isn't clear enough already, Elliot, I'll say it again. You may have bought the club but I'm not part of the furniture. You haven't bought *me*.'

'Zia...' Her name was a snake sound on his lips, sinister enough to make the hair on the nape of her neck rise. She shivered even before he touched her. His fingers were feather-light. When he spoke his voice was a mere whisper. 'I've already told you, if you want to break your contract, go ahead. See what happens.'

She froze. In an instant she saw she could risk everything and call his bluff. Or she could keep control of her instinctive anger at what he was doing to her and find another way out.

She turned on her chair to face him. 'I enjoy singing here. Why should I break my contract? But all I want to point out is, if someone is gallant enough to send me champagne and a single red rose every evening, that's my business, not yours. I shall, if I wish, accept a hundred red roses.'

'If you live long enough to be offered them.' He smiled without humour.

'That too.' She smiled a little as well.

Elliot, however, was only waiting for his moment. 'I intend to run this club as a respectable establishment, Zia. I don't wish to have my staff involved with the vice squad. If you step out of line I may have to issue a written warning to you.' He gave an arrogant jerk of the head as he turned to go.

Rachel stood up. 'How *dare* you?' She felt a violent race of colour scudding up her neck into her face. For a moment she felt she could literally see red. Before she could stop herself she had crossed the room and gripped him by the arm. As he turned she realised what she had done, but was powerless to release her hold on the sleeve of his dinner-jacket.

He looked down at her pale hand with its painted scarlet nails and rings of cheap coloured glass. On stage they looked exotic, but now they were what they were, a symbol of tawdry glamour. Time seemed to stop during which neither of them moved or spoke. Rachel was conscious of her own held breath. She was also intensely aware of the heady masculine scent of his cologne. It brought back memories of how he had once held her in his arms in a time that was now lost forever.

So slowly that she could count off the seconds, he lifted his own hand then grasped the offending one on his sleeve. With a gesture of deliberation he pushed it off. The space between them seemed to yawn like a chasm. To Rachel it seemed alive with criss-crossed wires, tugging and tearing apart the other lines that seemed to tie them together. It was all confusion. She couldn't turn away but nor could she go forward. She looked up. Elliot's blue eyes were fathomless, a deliberate professional blank.

Love me, Elliot, she found herself praying amid the tumult of her thoughts. But let me go, she prayed almost simultaneously. A small cry escaped her throat.

'You shouldn't have said that to me,' she heard herself say as if driven by the rules of convention to defend herself. 'You know it was uncalled for. As if I would——' she gasped '—as if I would behave like *that*!' She couldn't bring herself to say bluntly the thing he had accused her of. 'It's horrible of you, Elliot! You must know I'm not like that! You're deliberately trying to humiliate me. It's so unfair.' Her eyes seemed heavy with unshed tears but she was determined not to collapse in front of him. She tried to draw herself up. 'It shows exactly what you think of women in general to imagine, to even *imagine* such a thing!'

'Either you're blindly persisting in this role of naïve country girl, even though you know it's run its course and no longer convinces me, or you really do imagine you can carry on with my customers and never be called to book. Haven't I already told you—if you promise something, eventually someone is going to collect?'

Changing his mind about leaving, he kicked the door shut behind him and turned to her with a lethal smile. 'You flaunt your innocence by day, driving men wild with it. And on stage in the safety of the public eye you promise the tormenting pleasures of the night. Look but don't touch. Is it fair, Zia? Is it honest?'

'I don't—I don't do what you say!' she exclaimed. Something made her step back. 'I'm only singing. It's not my fault if men take my appearance to mean something else.'

'Are you so naïve?'

'Am I?' She looked bewildered.

He gave a harsh laugh. 'There it is again. That helpless, wide-eyed look. But you're not stupid, Zia. Not stupid by any means. You have a brain. You can't fail to know what sort of effect you're having. It's pure calculation.' He gave a groan. 'Hell, damn you! Why do I try to reason with you? We both know what game you're playing. Why can't I treat you with the contempt you deserve— or play along with it, like Henry?'

'Play along?'

'You don't imagine Henry doesn't know you're playing games, do you?'

'He's always very courteous——'

'Paws you a little, but nothing you can't control?'

'I suppose so, if you want to put it like that.'

'But that's his particular turn-on, isn't it, Zia? He likes the thrill of wondering how long it'll be before he can manoeuvre you into bed.'

'Don't be ridiculous, Elliot. He doesn't want that!'

'Stupid girl!' Elliot's face darkened. 'Every man in the audience wants that. Luckily most of them can't get near you. Ray used to make damn sure the barricade was up.'

'Ray?' She felt stupid now, only half understanding what he was saying.

'He warned me what would happen. "The stage-door johnny syndrome" he called it. He must have told you! He only allowed Henry to penetrate the security barrier because he thought it would take the pressure off if you could be seen with him now and then. Are you quite stupid?'

Rachel blinked. 'I'm only singing a few songs,' she muttered, turning away. 'You make it sound as if—I don't know.' She turned back. 'I don't know what I've done. I just——' She glanced briefly at her appearance in the wall-mirror. 'I just dress the part and go out and sing a few songs. I don't try to do anything else. I try to entertain. I just do——' She shrugged.

'Do what comes naturally?'

'Yes,' she said at once, then bit her lip again. It sounded bad like that.

His response was a harsh groan of sound wrenched from deep in his throat. 'Well, in case you still haven't realised it, Zia, what you think of as doing what comes naturally means only one thing to the chaps out there. And it has only one conclusion. I surely don't have to spell it out?'

She swallowed and shook her head.

'On the other hand,' he muttered thickly, 'perhaps a practical demonstration would help?'

He moved closer. 'Zia...' His breath was ragged. 'Damn you, Zia, for being such a tantalising little... I want——' His arms reached out for her before she could do more than bring up one hand in defence. Then she was enveloped in a hot embrace, her own body, aching with desire for him, overriding her natural impulse to resist. Betrayed by her own emotions, she clung to him, lifting her lips helplessly to receive his. His tongue swooped to meet her own, heat racing between them as all control deserted them.

There was a knock on the door.

Elliot dragged his lips away from their sweet plundering, his eyes bleared in confusion by this unexpected interruption. Rachel managed to tear herself out of his arms. She moved away, clutching the back of a chair to stem the violent shaking in her limbs.

'What is it?' Elliot's voice was rough-edged with anger. An apologetic Piers looked cautiously round the edge of the door. He had disposed of the champagne, but held the red rose in one hand.

'The reply, Zia,' he said, 'is, "please".' He took in Elliot's expression at once. 'Sorry, sir.'

'Give me that bloody rose.' Elliot snatched it out of his hand, tearing it into little pieces and throwing them savagely across the room. 'Tell him that! And if he persists, by God, I'll knock him down myself!'

Piers shot a startled glance at Rachel and went out, closing the door behind him with infinite caution.

'Bloody hell, Rachel, what do I have to do to keep you for myself? *Marry* you?'

She was still holding on to the back of the chair.

Elliot came towards her again and she flinched back as if she thought he was going to take hold of her again but instead he stood in front of her, raking one hand through his hair, eyes sweeping her flushed face with a look of dazed surprise.

'You won't be *bought*,' he muttered half to himself. He closed his eyes for an instant and she wondered what next. Already she felt as if she had spent the last half-hour on a roller-coaster that had spun out of control. Where it would fling her next she had no idea. All she could do was wait and see.

Elliot gave a sort of sigh and reached out with one hand to squeeze her waist. She tried not to flinch as he pressed with no apparent awareness of how hard he was handling her. Then he released her.

'Get ready to go home,' he said abruptly, swivelling towards the door.

With an effort she managed to prompt, 'Ray usually calls a cab for me. Fifteen minutes will do.'

He halted at the door and looked back. 'I'm not Ray, you'll get no cab from *me* . . .' He paused. 'I'll take you home myself.'

When he left she ran a shaking hand down her cheek. He was as disruptive as she suspected he would be at their very first meeting. She couldn't fight him. He seemed to attack her from all sides. The only thing she had to cling on to was that his accusations were one hundred per cent false. She had had no idea she affected men in the way he claimed.

By the time she was dressed in her plain wool coat and the make-up and the elaborate hairpiece were removed, she had come to a decision. Whether he liked it or not, from now on she would appear simply as Rachel. If it meant she was any less popular with the customers, then so be it. It wasn't right to pretend to be something she wasn't. The thought of what she had inadvertently done made her feel ill.

He stood in the corridor in a dark overcoat. The strip-light made his face seem haggard. There were lines of strain around his mouth.

'Ready?' He gave her a brief glance then looked again. 'Quite an actress, aren't you? Looking at you now, who'd believe you were Zia?'

He moved briskly towards the street door.

'I'm sorry, Elliot. I didn't realise.'

He gave her a scathing look, but when they were settled in his car she tried again. 'I had no idea you felt I was deliberately leading men on. It all seemed to begin by accident—the stage image, I mean. When I first started to sing I used to feel so horribly shy I wouldn't have dared go on without some sort of protective camouflage. It was while I was doing the window at the store I got the idea of borrowing one of the wigs from display.' She glanced quickly at him. 'I shouldn't have told you that. I don't want Lulu to get into trouble.'

'Don't worry about Lulu. Go on with what you're saying.'

'Well,' she continued, 'it just seemed to escalate from there. Obviously I couldn't wear a silver wig with a dull, plain dress. So I got something a bit flashy, in keeping with the Manhattan. It's a very stylish and exclusive place, isn't it?'

'Have you been to many clubs?' he asked.

'No. Actually, it's the only one.'

He gave a short laugh. 'Go on.'

'That's it, really. I felt I had to dress the part and it helped me get over my nerves. You've no idea, Elliot, how terrified I am before I go on. Even now after all this time.'

'All this time?' He took his eyes off the road for a moment. 'I know actors who've been treading the boards for a decade or more and still suffer stage fright.'

'That's it, then,' she said gloomily. 'I'm stuck with it.' Then she said, 'But if what you say is true—and I suppose it is—then I shall have to tone things down. It makes me feel horrible to think men imagine what you said about me. All I wanted was to look the part and sort of put the songs over as truthfully as I could.'

'And they are, after all, love-songs.'

She gave him a startled glance. He turned briefly and their eyes met.

'That's right, isn't it? Why do you look so surprised?'

'You sounded as if you almost understood,' she mumbled, looking down at her hands.

He pulled up at some traffic-lights. 'Either you're an even better actress than I thought or I've wronged you,' he said briefly. He drove on in silence.

When they reached her flat he switched off the engine. 'Don't worry, I'm not going to ask you if I can come in. I don't expect that.' He gazed out at the empty street. The sodium lights gave the trees and the fronts of the houses a poignant and strangely unreal beauty.

Rachel slumped. She felt drained and it was with an effort she turned to unlock her door.

'Don't go just yet.' His voice was gruff. 'Rachel——' He gave a short laugh. 'Rachel it is—and ever shall be,' he said somewhat enigmatically. 'Will you consider what I said to you in your dressing-room?' He didn't look at her.

'I've told you—I'm going to get rid of the fancy-dress.' She still felt pained that she could have laid herself open to his accusations. Scrabbling at the catch of the door, she got out of the car as quickly as she could and fled into the house.

Next morning she had come to a decision, hewn out of the restless hours of the night. She would back out of her contract at the club. There was really no alternative. If Elliot wanted to sue her then it was up to him—but if she explained her reasons he would surely understand.

What his words had done was point out something she should have realised long ago—that where her ambitions lay wasn't in nightclub singing at all, but in performance. The ease with which she had been able to slip in and out of the role of Zia should have shown her that at once, and the night at the opera had opened her eyes in more ways than one, confirming what she had begun to suspect. Of course she had no delusions about becoming an opera singer. Musicals were the avenue she wished to explore, and even if it meant singing in the back row of the chorus she knew she wouldn't be happy doing anything else. She would find a good teacher and learn the job properly. Then, perhaps, Elliot would realise what he had said about her leading men on had been untrue all along.

Even though they had no future together it was important to her that he should believe the best of her. To lose him hurt, but to have lost his respect hurt even more. She would rather he thought her a prude, with some sort of integrity, than a slut, with none.

On top of this she was going to confess something else to him when she told him the final goodbye—and it would only mean something if he knew he was the first man she had ever said it to.

She rang him at the store and left a message for him to ring her as soon as he was free. Then she practised a few songs from the musical while she waited.

It was less than half an hour later when he returned her call. 'I need to talk to you, Elliot. May we meet for lunch?' she asked without preamble.

He agreed to meet her in the West End.

Replacing the receiver she got up and went to her room. She dressed carefully in the dark suit with the white silk blouse and only the antique pin for adornment. Then she piled her sleek hair on top of her head and slipped into a pair of plain black court shoes. The final image was cool, professional and made her look far more composed than she felt. She took a taxi into town and arrived at their meeting place in good time.

He was already waiting and took her by the arm at once. 'You left without giving me your answer,' he muttered tersely. 'Is this it?'

She shot him a startled glance. 'It's about my contract,' she said, rushing to get the worst of it over. 'I want to break it.'

He stepped back, still holding her by the arm, his grasp tightening with involuntary force. His face looked almost grey. 'Let's get inside. We've got to talk first.'

He pushed her into the restaurant ahead of him. When they were seated he said gruffly, 'You've thought this through?'

'I tossed and turned all night long,' she admitted. 'There's no way out, but before you say anything, let me tell you why...' Briefly she outlined her reasons. 'You see,' she finished up when he had listened without interrupting, 'you're the first man I've ever loved and the only one I would ever give up my ambitions for—if it would make any difference.' She lowered her eyes to the cloth. 'I'm not saying that to make you feel bad or anything. I accept the fact that you don't want a serious relationship with anybody, with me least of all——' She tried to smile and raised her eyes then, through the tears that were suddenly swimming in them, she saw his face in front of her. But instead of looking bored or wearing any of the expected expressions he was smiling, with a look of such tenderness that she could only gulp and draw in a ragged breath. He was making it difficult for her, looking like that—as if he cared...

He didn't speak at once, but reached across the table for her hand. 'Idiot, idiot, idiot,' he repeated half to himself. 'Didn't you understand what I was saying to you last night?' He squeezed her hand. 'I said, "What do I have to do to keep you for myself, marry you?'' It wasn't the most orthodox proposal ever, but I certainly meant it to be taken seriously. I thought you were coming here today to give me your answer.'

When she went on staring at him in amazement he said, 'I accept your resignation from the club if you're sure that's what you want, so let's get on to this other question, shall we? What do you say about marrying me, Rachel? Is it yes—or no?'

Before she could recover from her astonishment he went on, 'I'd like us to have a proper engagement, a time when we can discover each other, rectify all past misunderstandings. I want to make you happy. And, Rachel, I want to see your ambition fulfilled too. When we first met you said something about not wanting to get involved because you were dedicated to your career. I go along with that. You have a very special talent, a rare and very moving talent as a performer. It would be a crime to clip your wings when you're just beginning to spread them. I want to help you.'

Rachel felt silent tears coursing down her cheeks and if anybody at the nearby tables noticed she didn't care because they were tears of happiness.

'I've loved you for so long,' she whispered, 'but I daren't admit how black life would seem without you. I tried to tell myself my career was all that mattered, because it would be permanent, while an affair with you wouldn't be. But Elliot, I've learned nothing matters except you. I love you so very much.'

He took both her hands in his. 'You seem to have forgotten what I told you about my time in the States when I was consultant to the music industry.

I guess I'm as highly qualified as anybody to manage your career. Now you've got into the habit of saying yes, maybe you'll say yes to a business partnership too? We could be the hottest duo on the scene. What do you say?'

'It's all too much and too fast, Elliot. I can't take it in. Just to be married to you would be enough.'

He gave a fond smile. 'I couldn't see your talent go to waste—it's part of the woman I love. You're going to be number one all the way—number one in my life and number one in the charts. Trust me, Rachel. I'm going to make it all happen the way you want it.'

Eyes enormous with emotion, Rachel could only gaze at him without speaking. After the storm that had preceded it this was such a complete reversal that it was as shattering as if night had turned instantly to day. But one small thing still bothered her. Eventually she managed to ask, 'When I threw myself at you that night in the hotel in Amsterdam, why didn't you——?' She blushed and bit her lip.

'Why didn't I follow my instincts?' He squeezed her hand. 'In a way I did. I knew if I made love to you then when you were determined to say goodbye you'd hate me forever, and it would fully convince you that I was the good-time Charlie you seemed to imagine. There was also something else. My spirit rebelled at taking you in anger. And after having the seal set on my suspicions, that's exactly what I felt that night. I thought you'd been trying to make a complete fool of me.'

'I'm sorry. It all got out of hand.'

'Don't worry. I'm in charge from now on. It won't happen again!'

With a small cry she reached across the table until their lips were touching. Oblivious to the waiters and the other diners, she said, 'Elliot, I love you. I thought I would never survive the loss of you— but I trapped myself in a situation I couldn't control. And now you've made my whole life perfect.'

'Is that yes and yes to both proposals?'

'Yes, Elliot, yes. I shall never be afraid that you'll turn my life upside-down again.'

'But I fully intend to,' he warned. 'You're going to be so successful, so famous, you can't imagine it.'

'To be honest,' she murmured against the side of his head, pressing her cheek against his beloved face, 'if you had pushed just a little bit more, I would have traded in all my dreams of fame to be with you. I hung on by the very tips of my fingers to the course I'd chosen because I thought you could never want me for keeps. If you only knew what it was like to have had to let you go,' she whispered.

'No need for sacrifices any more.' He pressed his lips gently against her eyelids. 'You can have everything your heart desires. I'm going to lay the world at your feet.'

Their engagement was announced in *The Times* two days later and then they did the rounds of parents and relatives. It was like a triumphal progress. Rachel was in a dream of happiness. Elliot was as perfect as she had all along known—and, in those first weeks, feared. But now there was no need to run from the impact he had on her life. Their paths were not in collision but ran side by side on the summit of happiness and fulfilment. Even when the producers of the musical she had auditioned for gave her a large role, Elliot was there, safeguarding her interests, organising Press interviews and getting much-needed publicity for her. He even managed to fix up her first recording contract. Herman Ward saw that Elliot meant business and was pleased to play his part without getting in his way. Besides, he had only signed Rachel for three months and knew it would be foolish to try to hang on.

It was with a hint of nostalgia that she came to sing for the last time at the Manhattan before leaving to start rehearsals for the musical. 'I hope you'll book me for a short guest season now and then, Elliot. I shall miss this old place. It reminds me so much of you.' She ran her fingers experimentally through his hair as they sat together at one of the tables while waiters bustled about preparing to open for the evening.

'I hope the place will be able to afford you. As your manager I'm not having you singing for nothing.'

'You're very tough.' She smiled.

'With a hot property like you to handle I have to be tough.' He smiled fondly as he caught her hand where it teased down the side of his neck. 'Though if you'd seen how I was quaking inside when I asked you to marry me you'd know I'm just a kitten at heart.'

'I love kittens,' she said.

'I love you,' he murmured, pressing his lips into the palm of her hand. Her eyes shone with love. She knew it was true. And would be so for the rest of time.

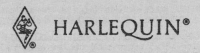

HARLEQUIN®

THE TAGGARTS OF TEXAS!

Harlequin's Ruth Jean Dale brings you
THE TAGGARTS OF TEXAS!

Those Taggart men—strong, sexy and hard to resist...

You've met Jesse James Taggart in FIREWORKS!
Harlequin Romance #3205 (July 1992)

And Trey Smith—he's THE RED-BLOODED YANKEE!
Harlequin Temptation #413 (October 1992)

Now meet Daniel Boone Taggart in SHOWDOWN!
Harlequin Romance #3242 (January 1993)

And finally the Taggarts who started it all—in LEGEND!
Harlequin Historical #168 (April 1993)

Read all the Taggart romances!
Meet all the Taggart men!

Available wherever Harlequin Books are sold.

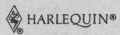

HARLEQUIN PRESENTS®

A Year
DOWN UNDER